T0143814

Lost Face

Lost Face

Jack London

MINT EDITIONS

Lost Face was first published in 1910.

This edition published by Mint Editions 2021.

ISBN 9781513206523 | E-ISBN 9781513275130

Published by Mint Editions®

 MINT EDITIONS

minteditionbooks.com

Publishing Director: Jennifer Newens
Design & Production: Rachel Lopez Metzger
Typesetting: Westchester Publishing Services

Contents

Lost Face

It was the end. Subienkow had travelled a long trail of bitterness and horror, homing like a dove for the capitals of Europe, and here, farther away than ever, in Russian America, the trail ceased. He sat in the snow, arms tied behind him, waiting the torture. He stared curiously before him at a huge Cossack, prone in the snow, moaning in his pain. The men had finished handling the giant and turned him over to the women. That they exceeded the fiendishness of the men, the man's cries attested.

Subienkow looked on, and shuddered. He was not afraid to die. He had carried his life too long in his hands, on that weary trail from Warsaw to Nulato, to shudder at mere dying. But he objected to the torture. It offended his soul. And this offence, in turn, was not due to the mere pain he must endure, but to the sorry spectacle the pain would make of him. He knew that he would pray, and beg, and entreat, even as Big Ivan and the others that had gone before. This would not be nice. To pass out bravely and cleanly, with a smile and a jest—ah! that would have been the way. But to lose control, to have his soul upset by the pangs of the flesh, to screech and gibber like an ape, to become the veriest beast—ah, that was what was so terrible.

There had been no chance to escape. From the beginning, when he dreamed the fiery dream of Poland's independence, he had become a puppet in the hands of Fate. From the beginning, at Warsaw, at St. Petersburg, in the Siberian mines, in Kamtchatka, on the crazy boats of the fur-thieves, Fate had been driving him to this end. Without doubt, in the foundations of the world was graved this end for him—for him, who was so fine and sensitive, whose nerves scarcely sheltered under his skin, who was a dreamer, and a poet, and an artist. Before he was dreamed of, it had been determined that the quivering bundle of sensitiveness that constituted him should be doomed to live in raw and howling savagery, and to die in this far land of night, in this dark place beyond the last boundaries of the world.

He sighed. So that thing before him was Big Ivan—Big Ivan the giant, the man without nerves, the man of iron, the Cossack turned freebooter of the seas, who was as phlegmatic as an ox, with a nervous system so low that what was pain to ordinary men was scarcely a tickle to him. Well, well, trust these Nulato Indians to find Big Ivan's nerves and trace them to the roots of his quivering soul. They were certainly doing it. It was inconceivable that a man could suffer so much and yet live. Big Ivan was paying for his low order of nerves. Already he had lasted twice as long as any of the others.

Subienkow felt that he could not stand the Cossack's sufferings much longer. Why didn't Ivan die? He would go mad if that screaming did not cease. But when it did cease, his turn would come. And there was Yakaga awaiting him, too, grinning at him even now in anticipation—Yakaga, whom only last week he had kicked out of the fort, and upon whose face he had laid the lash of his dog-whip. Yakaga would attend to him. Doubtlessly Yakaga was saving for him more refined tortures, more exquisite nerve-racking. Ah! that must have been a good one, from the way Ivan screamed. The squaws bending over him stepped back with laughter and clapping of hands. Subienkow saw the monstrous thing that had been perpetrated, and began to laugh hysterically. The Indians looked at him in wonderment that he should laugh. But Subienkow could not stop.

This would never do. He controlled himself, the spasmodic twitchings slowly dying away. He strove to think of other things, and began reading back in his own life. He remembered his mother and his father, and the little spotted pony, and the French tutor who had taught him dancing and sneaked him an old worn copy of Voltaire. Once more he saw Paris, and dreary London, and gay Vienna, and Rome. And once more he saw that wild group of youths who had dreamed, even as he, the dream of an independent Poland with a king of Poland on the throne at Warsaw. Ah, there it was that the long trail began. Well, he had lasted longest. One by one, beginning with the two executed at St. Petersburg, he took up the count of the passing of those brave spirits. Here one had been beaten to death by a jailer, and there, on that bloodstained highway of the exiles, where they had marched for endless months, beaten and maltreated by their Cossack guards, another had dropped by the way. Always it had been savagery—brutal, bestial savagery. They had died—of fever, in the mines, under the knout. The last two had died after the escape, in the battle with the Cossacks, and he alone had won to Kamtchatka with the stolen papers and the money of a traveller he had left lying in the snow.

It had been nothing but savagery. All the years, with his heart in studios, and theatres, and courts, he had been hemmed in by savagery. He had purchased his life with blood. Everybody had killed. He had killed that traveller for his passports. He had proved that he was a man of parts by duelling with two Russian officers on a single day. He had had to prove himself in order to win to a place among the fur-thieves. He had had to win to that place. Behind him lay the thousand-years-long road across all Siberia and Russia. He could not escape that way. The only way was ahead, across the dark and icy sea of Bering to Alaska. The way had led from savagery to deeper savagery. On the scurvy-rotten ships of the fur-thieves, out of food and out of water, buffeted by the interminable storms of that stormy sea, men had become animals. Thrice he had sailed east from Kamtchatka. And thrice, after all manner of hardship and suffering, the survivors had come back to Kamtchatka. There had been no outlet for escape, and he could not go back the way he had come, for the mines and the knout awaited him.

Again, the fourth and last time, he had sailed east. He had been with those who first found the fabled Seal Islands; but he had not returned with them to share the wealth of furs in the mad orgies of Kamtchatka. He had sworn never to go back. He knew that to win to those dear capitals of Europe he must go on. So he had changed ships and remained in the dark new land. His comrades were Slavonian hunters and Russian adventurers, Mongols and Tartars and Siberian aborigines; and through the savages of the new world they had cut a path of blood. They had massacred whole villages that refused to furnish the fur-tribute; and they, in turn, had been massacred by ships' companies. He, with one Finn, had been the sole survivor of such a company. They had spent a winter of solitude and starvation on a lonely Aleutian isle, and their rescue in the spring by another fur-ship had been one chance in a thousand.

But always the terrible savagery had hemmed him in. Passing from ship to ship, and ever refusing to return, he had come to the ship that explored south. All down the Alaska coast they had encountered nothing but hosts of savages. Every anchorage among the beetling islands or under the frowning cliffs of the mainland had meant a battle or a storm. Either the gales blew, threatening destruction, or the war canoes came off, manned by howling natives with the war-paint on their faces, who came to learn the bloody virtues of the sea-rovers' gunpowder. South, south they had coasted, clear to the myth-land of California. Here, it was said, were Spanish adventurers who had fought their way up from Mexico. He had had hopes of those Spanish adventurers. Escaping to them, the rest would have been easy—a year or two, what did it matter more or less—and he would win to Mexico, then a ship, and Europe would be his. But they had met no Spaniards. Only had they encountered the same impregnable wall of savagery. The denizens of the confines of the world, painted for war, had driven them back from the shores. At last, when one boat was cut off and every man killed, the commander had abandoned the quest and sailed back to the north.

The years had passed. He had served under Tebenkoff when Michaelovski Redoubt was built. He had spent two years in the Kuskokwim country. Two summers, in the month of June, he had managed to be at the head of Kotzebue Sound. Here, at this time, the tribes assembled for barter; here were to be found spotted deerskins from Siberia, ivory from the Diomedes, walrus skins from the shores of the Arctic, strange stone lamps, passing in trade from tribe to tribe, no one knew whence, and, once, a hunting-knife of English make; and here, Subienkow knew, was the school in which to learn geography. For he met Eskimos from Norton Sound, from King Island and St. Lawrence Island, from Cape Prince of Wales, and Point Barrow. Such places had other names, and their distances were measured in days.

It was a vast region these trading savages came from, and a vaster region from which, by repeated trade, their stone lamps and that steel knife had come. Subienkow bullied, and cajoled, and bribed. Every far-journeyer or strange tribesman was brought before him. Perils unaccountable and unthinkable were mentioned, as well as wild beasts, hostile tribes, impenetrable forests, and mighty mountain ranges; but always from beyond came the rumour and the tale of white-skinned men, blue of eye and fair of hair, who fought like devils and who sought always for furs. They were to the east—far, far to the east. No one had seen them. It was the word that had been passed along.

It was a hard school. One could not learn geography very well through the medium of strange dialects, from dark minds that mingled fact and fable and that measured distances by "sleeps" that varied according to the difficulty of the going. But at last came the whisper that gave Subienkow courage. In the east lay a great river where were these blue-eyed men. The river was called the Yukon. South of Michaelovski Redoubt emptied another great river which the Russians knew as the Kwikpak. These two rivers were one, ran the whisper.

Subienkow returned to Michaelovski. For a year he urged an expedition up the Kwikpak. Then arose Malakoff, the Russian half-breed, to lead the wildest and most ferocious of the hell's broth of mongrel adventurers who had crossed from Kamtchatka. Subienkow was his lieutenant. They threaded the mazes of the great delta of the Kwikpak, picked up the first low hills on the northern bank, and for half a thousand miles, in skin canoes loaded to the gunwales with trade-goods and ammunition, fought their way against the five-knot current of a river that ran from two to ten miles wide in a channel many fathoms deep. Malakoff decided to build the fort at Nulato. Subienkow urged to go farther. But he quickly reconciled himself to Nulato. The long winter was coming on. It would be better to wait. Early the following summer, when the ice was gone, he would disappear up the Kwikpak and work his way to the Hudson Bay Company's posts. Malakoff had never heard the whisper that the Kwikpak was the Yukon, and Subienkow did not tell him.

Came the building of the fort. It was enforced labour. The tiered walls of logs arose to the sighs and groans of the Nulato Indians. The lash was laid upon their backs, and it was the iron hand of the freebooters of the sea that laid on the lash. There were Indians that ran away, and when they were caught they were brought back and spread-eagled before the fort, where they and their tribe learned the efficacy of the knout. Two died under it; others were injured for life; and the rest took the lesson to heart and ran away no more. The snow was flying ere the fort was finished, and then it was the time for furs. A heavy tribute was laid upon the tribe. Blows and lashings continued, and that the tribute should be paid, the women and children were held as hostages and treated with the barbarity that only the fur-thieves knew.

Well, it had been a sowing of blood, and now was come the harvest. The fort was gone. In the light of its burning, half the fur-thieves had been cut down. The other half had passed under the torture. Only Subienkow remained, or Subienkow and Big Ivan, if that whimpering, moaning thing in the snow could be called Big Ivan. Subienkow caught Yakaga grinning at him. There was no gainsaying Yakaga. The mark of the lash was still on his face. After all, Subienkow could not blame him, but he disliked the thought of what Yakaga would do to him. He thought of appealing to Makamuk, the head-chief; but his judgment told him that such appeal was useless. Then, too, he thought of bursting his bonds and dying fighting. Such an end would be quick. But he could not break his bonds. Caribou thongs were stronger than he. Still devising, another thought came to him. He signed for Makamuk, and that an interpreter who knew the coast dialect should be brought.

"Oh, Makamuk," he said, "I am not minded to die. I am a great man, and it were foolishness for me to die. In truth, I shall not die. I am not like these other carrion."

He looked at the moaning thing that had once been Big Ivan, and stirred it contemptuously with his toe.

"I am too wise to die. Behold, I have a great medicine. I alone know this medicine. Since I am not going to die, I shall exchange this medicine with you."

"What is this medicine?" Makamuk demanded.

"It is a strange medicine."

Subienkow debated with himself for a moment, as if loth to part with the secret.

"I will tell you. A little bit of this medicine rubbed on the skin makes the skin hard like a rock, hard like iron, so that no cutting weapon can cut it. The strongest blow of a cutting weapon is a vain thing against it. A bone knife becomes like a piece of mud; and it will turn the edge of the iron knives we have brought among you. What will you give me for the secret of the medicine?"

"I will give you your life," Makamuk made answer through the interpreter.

Subienkow laughed scornfully.

"And you shall be a slave in my house until you die."

The Pole laughed more scornfully.

"Untie my hands and feet and let us talk," he said.

The chief made the sign; and when he was loosed Subienkow rolled a cigarette and lighted it.

"This is foolish talk," said Makamuk. "There is no such medicine. It cannot be. A cutting edge is stronger than any medicine."

The chief was incredulous, and yet he wavered. He had seen too many deviltries of fur-thieves that worked. He could not wholly doubt.

"I will give you your life; but you shall not be a slave," he announced. "More than that."

Subienkow played his game as coolly as if he were bartering for a foxskin.

"It is a very great medicine. It has saved my life many times. I want a sled and dogs, and six of your hunters to travel with me down the river and give me safety to one day's sleep from Michaelovski Redoubt."

"You must live here, and teach us all of your deviltries," was the reply.

Subienkow shrugged his shoulders and remained silent. He blew cigarette smoke out on the icy air, and curiously regarded what remained of the big Cossack.

"That scar!" Makamuk said suddenly, pointing to the Pole's neck, where a livid mark advertised the slash of a knife in a Kamtchatkan brawl. "The medicine is not good. The cutting edge was stronger than the medicine."

"It was a strong man that drove the stroke." (Subienkow considered.) "Stronger than you, stronger than your strongest hunter, stronger than he."

Again, with the toe of his moccasin, he touched the Cossack—a grisly spectacle, no longer conscious—yet in whose dismembered body the pain-racked life clung and was loth to go.

"Also, the medicine was weak. For at that place there were no berries of a certain kind, of which I see you have plenty in this country. The medicine here will be strong."

"I will let you go down river," said Makamuk; "and the sled and the dogs and the six hunters to give you safety shall be yours."

"You are slow," was the cool rejoinder. "You have committed an offence against my medicine in that you did not at once accept my terms. Behold, I now demand more. I want one hundred beaver skins." (Makamuk sneered.)

"I want one hundred pounds of dried fish." (Makamuk nodded, for fish were plentiful and cheap.) "I want two sleds—one for me and one for my furs and fish. And my rifle must be returned to me. If you do not like the price, in a little while the price will grow."

Yakaga whispered to the chief.

"But how can I know your medicine is true medicine?" Makamuk asked.

"It is very easy. First, I shall go into the woods—"

Again Yakaga whispered to Makamuk, who made a suspicious dissent.

"You can send twenty hunters with me," Subienkow went on. "You see, I must get the berries and the roots with which to make the medicine. Then, when you have brought the two sleds and loaded on them the fish and the beaver skins and the rifle, and when you have told off the six hunters who will go with me—then, when all is ready, I will rub the medicine on my neck, so, and lay my neck there on that log. Then can your strongest hunter take the axe and strike three times on my neck. You yourself can strike the three times."

Makamuk stood with gaping mouth, drinking in this latest and most wonderful magic of the fur-thieves.

"But first," the Pole added hastily, "between each blow I must put on fresh medicine. The axe is heavy and sharp, and I want no mistakes."

"All that you have asked shall be yours," Makamuk cried in a rush of acceptance. "Proceed to make your medicine."

Subienkow concealed his elation. He was playing a desperate game, and there must be no slips. He spoke arrogantly.

"You have been slow. My medicine is offended. To make the offence clean you must give me your daughter."

He pointed to the girl, an unwholesome creature, with a cast in one eye and a bristling wolf-tooth. Makamuk was angry, but the Pole remained imperturbable, rolling and lighting another cigarette.

"Make haste," he threatened. "If you are not quick, I shall demand yet more."

In the silence that followed, the dreary northland scene faded before him, and he saw once more his native land, and France, and, once, as he glanced at the wolf-toothed girl, he remembered another girl, a singer and a dancer, whom he had known when first as a youth he came to Paris.

"What do you want with the girl?" Makamuk asked.

"To go down the river with me." Subienkow glanced over her critically. "She will make a good wife, and it is an honour worthy of my medicine to be married to your blood."

Again he remembered the singer and dancer and hummed aloud a song she had taught him. He lived the old life over, but in a detached, impersonal sort of way, looking at the memory-pictures of his own life as if they were pictures in a book of anybody's life. The chief's voice, abruptly breaking the silence, startled him

"It shall be done," said Makamuk. "The girl shall go down the river with you. But be it understood that I myself strike the three blows with the axe on your neck."

"But each time I shall put on the medicine," Subienkow answered, with a show of ill-concealed anxiety.

"You shall put the medicine on between each blow. Here are the hunters who shall see you do not escape. Go into the forest and gather your medicine."

Makamuk had been convinced of the worth of the medicine by the Pole's rapacity. Surely nothing less than the greatest of medicines could enable a man in the shadow of death to stand up and drive an old-woman's bargain.

"Besides," whispered Yakaga, when the Pole, with his guard, had disappeared among the spruce trees, "when you have learned the medicine you can easily destroy him."

"But how can I destroy him?" Makamuk argued. "His medicine will not let me destroy him."

"There will be some part where he has not rubbed the medicine," was Yakaga's reply. "We will destroy him through that part. It may be his ears. Very well; we will thrust a spear in one ear and out the other. Or it may be his eyes. Surely the medicine will be much too strong to rub on his eyes."

The chief nodded. "You are wise, Yakaga. If he possesses no other devil-things, we will then destroy him."

Subienkow did not waste time in gathering the ingredients for his medicine, he selected whatsoever came to hand such as spruce needles, the inner bark of the willow, a strip of birch bark, and a quantity of moss-berries, which he made the hunters dig up for him from beneath the snow. A few frozen roots completed his supply, and he led the way back to camp.

Makamuk and Yakaga crouched beside him, noting the quantities and kinds of the ingredients he dropped into the pot of boiling water.

"You must be careful that the moss-berries go in first," he explained.

"And—oh, yes, one other thing—the finger of a man. Here, Yakaga, let me cut off your finger."

But Yakaga put his hands behind him and scowled.

"Just a small finger," Subienkow pleaded.

"Yakaga, give him your finger," Makamuk commanded.

"There be plenty of fingers lying around," Yakaga grunted, indicating the human wreckage in the snow of the score of persons who had been tortured to death.

"It must be the finger of a live man," the Pole objected.

"Then shall you have the finger of a live man." Yakaga strode over to the Cossack and sliced off a finger.

"He is not yet dead," he announced, flinging the bloody trophy in the snow at the Pole's feet. "Also, it is a good finger, because it is large."

Subienkow dropped it into the fire under the pot and began to sing. It was a French love-song that with great solemnity he sang into the brew.

"Without these words I utter into it, the medicine is worthless," he explained. "The words are the chiefest strength of it. Behold, it is ready."

"Name the words slowly, that I may know them," Makamuk commanded.

"Not until after the test. When the axe flies back three times from my neck, then will I give you the secret of the words."

"But if the medicine is not good medicine?" Makamuk queried anxiously.

Subienkow turned upon him wrathfully.

"My medicine is always good. However, if it is not good, then do by me as you have done to the others. Cut me up a bit at a time, even as you have cut him up." He pointed to the Cossack. "The medicine is now cool. Thus, I rub it on my neck, saying this further medicine."

With great gravity he slowly intoned a line of the "Marseillaise," at the same time rubbing the villainous brew thoroughly into his neck.

An outcry interrupted his play-acting. The giant Cossack, with a last resurgence of his tremendous vitality, had arisen to his knees. Laughter and cries of surprise and applause arose from the Nulatos, as Big Ivan began flinging himself about in the snow with mighty spasms.

Subienkow was made sick by the sight, but he mastered his qualms and made believe to be angry.

"This will not do," he said. "Finish him, and then we will make the test. Here, you, Yakaga, see that his noise ceases."

While this was being done, Subienkow turned to Makamuk.

"And remember, you are to strike hard. This is not baby-work. Here, take the axe and strike the log, so that I can see you strike like a man."

Makamuk obeyed, striking twice, precisely and with vigour, cutting out a large chip.

"It is well." Subienkow looked about him at the circle of savage faces that somehow seemed to symbolize the wall of savagery that had hemmed him about ever since the Czar's police had first arrested him in Warsaw. "Take your axe, Makamuk, and stand so. I shall lie down. When I raise my hand, strike, and strike with all your might. And be careful that no one stands behind you. The medicine is good, and the axe may bounce from off my neck and right out of your hands."

He looked at the two sleds, with the dogs in harness, loaded with furs and fish. His rifle lay on top of the beaver skins. The six hunters who were to act as his guard stood by the sleds.

"Where is the girl?" the Pole demanded. "Bring her up to the sleds before the test goes on."

When this had been carried out, Subienkow lay down in the snow, resting his head on the log like a tired child about to sleep. He had lived so many dreary years that he was indeed tired.

"I laugh at you and your strength, O Makamuk," he said. "Strike, and strike hard."

He lifted his hand. Makamuk swung the axe, a broadaxe for the squaring of logs. The bright steel flashed through the frosty air, poised for a perceptible instant above Makamuk's head, then descended upon Subienkow's bare neck. Clear through flesh and bone it cut its way, biting deeply into the log beneath. The amazed savages saw the head bounce a yard away from the blood-spouting trunk.

There was a great bewilderment and silence, while slowly it began to dawn in their minds that there had been no medicine. The fur-thief had outwitted them. Alone, of all their prisoners, he had escaped the torture. That had been the stake for which he played. A great roar of laughter went up. Makamuk bowed his head in shame. The fur-thief had fooled him. He had lost face before all his people. Still they continued to roar out their laughter. Makamuk turned, and with bowed head stalked away. He knew that thenceforth he would be no longer known as Makamuk. He would be Lost Face; the record of his shame would be with him until he died; and whenever the tribes gathered in the spring for the salmon, or in the summer for the trading, the story would pass back and forth across the camp-fires of how the fur-thief died peaceably, at a single stroke, by the hand of Lost Face.

"Who was Lost Face?" he could hear, in anticipation, some insolent young buck demand, "Oh, Lost Face," would be the answer, "he who once was Makamuk in the days before he cut off the fur-thief's head."

Trust

A ll lines had been cast off, and the *Seattle No.* 4 was pulling slowly out from the shore. Her decks were piled high with freight and baggage, and swarmed with a heterogeneous company of Indians, dogs, and dog-mushers, prospectors, traders, and homeward-bound gold-seekers. A goodly portion of Dawson was lined up on the bank, saying good-bye. As the gang-plank came in and the steamer nosed into the stream, the clamour of farewell became deafening. Also, in that eleventh moment, everybody began to remember final farewell messages and to shout them back and forth across the widening stretch of water. Louis Bondell, curling his yellow moustache with one hand and languidly waving the other hand to his friends on shore, suddenly remembered something and sprang to the rail.

"Oh, Fred!" he bawled. "Oh, Fred!"

The "Fred" desired thrust a strapping pair of shoulders through the forefront of the crowd on the bank and tried to catch Louis Bondell's message. The latter grew red in the face with vain vociferation. Still the water widened between steamboat and shore.

"Hey, you, Captain Scott!" he yelled at the pilot-house. "Stop the boat!"

The gongs clanged, and the big stern wheel reversed, then stopped. All hands on steamboat and on bank took advantage of this respite to exchange final, new, and imperative farewells. More futile than ever was Louis Bondell's effort to make himself heard. The *Seattle No.* 4 lost way and drifted down-stream, and Captain Scott had to go ahead and reverse a second time. His head disappeared inside the pilot-house, coming into view a moment later behind a big megaphone.

Now Captain Scott had a remarkable voice, and the "Shut up!" he launched at the crowd on deck and on shore could have been heard at the top of Moosehide Mountain and as far as Klondike City. This official remonstrance from the pilot-house spread a film of silence over the tumult.

"Now, what do you want to say?" Captain Scott demanded.

"Tell Fred Churchill—he's on the bank there—tell him to go to Macdonald. It's in his safe—a small gripsack of mine. Tell him to get it and bring it out when he comes."

In the silence Captain Scott bellowed the message ashore through the megaphone:—

"You, Fred Churchill, go to Macdonald—in his safe—small gripsack—belongs to Louis Bondell—important! Bring it out when you come! Got it!"

Churchill waved his hand in token that he had got it. In truth, had Macdonald, half a mile away, opened his window, he'd have got it, too. The tumult of farewell rose again, the gongs clanged, and the *Seattle No. 4* went ahead, swung out into the stream, turned on her heel, and headed down the Yukon, Bondell and Churchill waving farewell and mutual affection to the last.

That was in midsummer. In the fall of the year, the *W. H. Willis* started up the Yukon with two hundred homeward-bound pilgrims on board. Among them was Churchill. In his state-room, in the middle of a clothes-bag, was Louis Bondell's grip. It was a small, stout leather affair, and its weight of forty pounds always made Churchill nervous when he wandered too far from it. The man in the adjoining state-room had a treasure of gold-dust hidden similarly in a clothes-bag, and the pair of them ultimately arranged to stand watch and watch. While one went down to eat, the other kept an eye on the two state-room doors. When Churchill wanted to take a hand at whist, the other man mounted guard, and when the other man wanted to relax his soul, Churchill read four-months' old newspapers on a camp stool between the two doors.

There were signs of an early winter, and the question that was discussed from dawn till dark, and far into the dark, was whether they would get out before the freeze-up or be compelled to abandon the steamboat and tramp out over the ice. There were irritating delays. Twice the engines broke down and had to be tinkered up, and each time there were snow flurries to warn them of the imminence of winter. Nine times the *W. H. Willis* essayed to ascend the Five-Finger Rapids with her impaired machinery, and when she succeeded, she was four days behind her very liberal schedule. The question that then arose was whether or not the steamboat *Flora* would wait for her above the Box Cañon. The stretch of water between the head of the Box Cañon and the foot of the White Horse Rapids was unnavigable for steamboats, and passengers were transhipped at that point, walking around the rapids from one steamboat to the other. There were no telephones in the country, hence no way of informing the waiting *Flora* that the *Willis* was four days late, but coming.

When the *W. H. Willis* pulled into White Horse, it was learned that the *Flora* had waited three days over the limit, and had departed only a few hours before. Also, it was learned that she would tie up at Tagish Post till nine o'clock, Sunday morning. It was then four o'clock, Saturday afternoon. The pilgrims called a meeting. On board was a large Peterborough canoe, consigned to the police post at the head of Lake Bennett. They agreed to be responsible for it and to deliver it. Next, they called for volunteers. Two men were needed to make a race for the *Flora*. A score of men volunteered on the instant. Among them was Churchill, such being his nature that he volunteered before he thought of Bondell's gripsack. When this thought came to him, he began to hope that he would not be selected; but a man who had made a name as captain of a college football eleven, as a president of an athletic club, as a dog-musher and a stampeder in the Yukon, and, moreover, who possessed such shoulders as he, had no right to avoid the honour. It was thrust upon him and upon a gigantic German, Nick Antonsen.

While a crowd of the pilgrims, the canoe on their shoulders, started on a trot over the portage, Churchill ran to his state-room. He turned the contents of the clothes-bag on the floor and caught up the grip, with the intention of entrusting it to the man next door. Then the thought smote him that it was not his grip, and that he had no right to let it out of his possession. So he dashed ashore with it and ran up the portage changing it often from one hand to the other, and wondering if it really did not weigh more than forty pounds.

It was half-past four in the afternoon when the two men started. The current of the Thirty Mile River was so strong that rarely could they use the paddles. It was out on one bank with a tow-line over the shoulders, stumbling over the rocks, forcing a way through the underbrush, slipping at times and falling into the water, wading often up to the knees and waist; and then, when an insurmountable bluff was encountered, it was into the canoe, out paddles, and a wild and losing dash across the current to the other bank, in paddles, over the side, and out tow-line again. It was exhausting work. Antonsen toiled like the giant he was, uncomplaining, persistent, but driven to his utmost by the powerful body and indomitable brain of Churchill. They never paused for rest. It was go, go, and keep on going. A crisp wind blew down the river, freezing their hands and making it imperative, from time to time, to beat the blood back into the numbed fingers.

As night came on, they were compelled to trust to luck. They fell repeatedly on the untravelled banks and tore their clothing to shreds in the underbrush they could not see. Both men were badly scratched and bleeding. A dozen times, in their wild dashes from bank to bank, they struck snags and were capsized. The first time this happened, Churchill dived and groped in three feet of water for the gripsack. He lost half an hour in recovering it, and after that it was carried securely lashed to the canoe. As long as the canoe floated it was safe. Antonsen jeered at the grip, and toward morning began to curse it; but Churchill vouchsafed no explanations.

Their delays and mischances were endless. On one swift bend, around which poured a healthy young rapid, they lost two hours, making a score of attempts and capsizing twice. At this point, on both banks, were precipitous bluffs, rising out of deep water, and along which they could neither tow nor pole, while they could not gain with the paddles against the current. At each attempt they strained to the utmost with the paddles, and each time, with heads nigh to bursting from the effort, they were played out and swept back. They succeeded finally by an accident. In the swiftest current, near the end of another failure, a freak of the current sheered the canoe out of Churchill's control and flung it against the bluff. Churchill made a blind leap at the bluff and landed in a crevice. Holding on with one hand, he held the swamped canoe with the other till Antonsen dragged himself out of the water. Then they pulled the canoe out and rested. A fresh start at this crucial point took them by. They landed on the bank above and plunged immediately ashore and into the brush with the tow-line.

Daylight found them far below Tagish Post. At nine o'clock Sunday morning they could hear the *Flora* whistling her departure. And when, at ten o'clock, they dragged themselves in to the Post, they could barely see the *Flora's* smoke far to the southward. It was a pair of worn-out tatterdemalions that Captain Jones of the Mounted Police welcomed and fed, and he afterward averred that they possessed two of the most tremendous appetites he had ever observed. They lay down and slept in their wet rags by the stove. At the end of two hours Churchill got up, carried Bondell's grip, which he had used for a pillow, down to the canoe, kicked Antonsen awake, and started in pursuit of the *Flora*.

"There's no telling what might happen—machinery break down, or something," was his reply to Captain Jones's expostulations. "I'm going to catch that steamer and send her back for the boys."

Tagish Lake was white with a fall gale that blew in their teeth. Big, swinging seas rushed upon the canoe, compelling one man to bale and leaving one man to paddle. Headway could not be made. They ran along the shallow shore and went overboard, one man ahead on the tow-line, the other shoving on the canoe. They fought the gale up to their waists in the icy water, often up to their necks, often over their heads and buried by the big, crested waves. There was no rest, never a moment's pause from the cheerless, heart-breaking battle. That night, at the head of Tagish Lake, in the thick of a driving snow-squall, they overhauled the *Flora*. Antonsen fell on board, lay where he had fallen, and snored. Churchill looked like a wild man. His clothes barely clung to him. His face was iced up and swollen from the protracted effort of twenty-four hours, while his hands were so swollen that he could not close the fingers. As for his feet, it was an agony to stand upon them.

The captain of the *Flora* was loth to go back to White Horse. Churchill was persistent and imperative; the captain was stubborn. He pointed out finally that nothing was to be gained by going back, because the only ocean steamer at Dyea, the *Athenian*, was to sail on Tuesday morning, and that he could not make the back trip to White Horse and bring up the stranded pilgrims in time to make the connection.

"What time does the *Athenian* sail?" Churchill demanded.

"Seven o'clock, Tuesday morning."

"All right," Churchill said, at the same time kicking a tattoo on the ribs of the snoring Antonsen. "You go back to White Home. We'll go ahead and hold the *Athenian*."

Antonsen, stupid with sleep, not yet clothed in his waking mind, was bundled into the canoe, and did not realize what had happened till he was drenched with the icy spray of a big sea, and heard Churchill snarling at him through the darkness:—

"Paddle, can't you! Do you want to be swamped?"

Daylight found them at Caribou Crossing, the wind dying down, and Antonsen too far gone to dip a paddle. Churchill grounded the canoe on a quiet beach, where they slept. He took the precaution of twisting his arm under the weight of his head. Every few minutes the pain of the pent circulation aroused him, whereupon he would look at his watch and twist the other arm under his head. At the end of two hours he fought with Antonsen to rouse him. Then they started. Lake Bennett, thirty miles in length, was like a millpond; but, half way across, a gale from the south smote them and turned the water white. Hour after hour they repeated the struggle on Tagish, over the side, pulling and shoving on the canoe, up to their waists and necks, and over their heads, in the icy water; toward the last the good-natured giant played completely out. Churchill drove him mercilessly; but when he pitched forward and bade fair to drown in three feet of water, the other dragged him into the canoe. After that, Churchill fought on alone, arriving at the police post at the head of Bennett in the early afternoon. He tried to help Antonsen out of the canoe, but failed. He listened to the exhausted man's heavy breathing, and envied him when he thought of what he himself had yet to undergo. Antonsen could lie there and sleep; but he, behind time, must go on over mighty Chilcoot and down to the sea. The real struggle lay before him, and he almost regretted the strength that resided in his frame because of the torment it could inflict upon that frame.

Churchill pulled the canoe up on the beach, seized Bondell's grip, and started on a limping dog-trot for the police post.

"There's a canoe down there, consigned to you from Dawson," he hurled at the officer who answered his knock. "And there's a man in it pretty near dead. Nothing serious; only played out. Take care of him. I've got to rush. Good-bye. Want to catch the *Athenian*."

A mile portage connected Lake Bennett and Lake Linderman, and his last words he flung back after him as he resumed the trot. It was a very painful trot, but he clenched his teeth and kept on, forgetting his pain most of the time in the fervent heat with which he regarded the gripsack. It was a severe handicap. He swung it from one hand to the other, and back again. He tucked it under his arm. He threw one hand over the opposite shoulder, and the bag bumped and pounded on his back as he ran along. He could scarcely hold it in his bruised and swollen fingers, and several times he dropped it. Once, in changing from one hand to the other, it escaped his clutch and fell in front of him, tripped him up, and threw him violently to the ground.

At the far end of the portage he bought an old set of pack-straps for a dollar, and in them he swung the grip. Also, he chartered a launch to run him the six miles to the upper end of Lake Linderman, where he arrived at four in the afternoon. The *Athenian* was to sail from Dyea next morning at seven. Dyea was twenty-eight miles away, and between towered Chilcoot. He sat down to adjust his foot-gear for the long climb, and woke up. He had dozed the instant he sat down, though he had not slept thirty seconds. He was afraid his next doze might be longer, so he finished fixing his foot-gear standing up. Even then he was overpowered for a fleeting moment. He experienced the flash of unconsciousness; becoming aware of it, in mid-air, as his relaxed body was sinking to the ground and as he caught himself together, he stiffened his muscles with a spasmodic wrench, and escaped the fall. The sudden jerk back to consciousness left him sick and trembling. He beat his head with the heel of his hand, knocking wakefulness into the numbed brain.

Jack Burns's pack-train was starting back light for Crater Lake, and Churchill was invited to a mule. Burns wanted to put the gripsack on another animal, but Churchill held on to it, carrying it on his saddle-pommel. But he dozed, and the grip persisted in dropping off the pommel, one side or the other, each time wakening him with a sickening start. Then, in the early darkness, Churchill's mule brushed him against a projecting branch that laid his cheek open. To cap it, the mule blundered off the trail and fell, throwing rider and gripsack out upon the rocks. After that, Churchill walked, or stumbled rather, over the apology for a trail, leading the mule. Stray and awful odours, drifting from each side of the trail, told of the horses that had died in the rush for gold. But he did not mind. He was too sleepy. By the time Long Lake was reached, however, he had recovered from his sleepiness; and at Deep Lake he resigned the gripsack to Burns. But thereafter, by the light of the dim stars, he kept his eyes on Burns. There were not going to be any accidents with that bag.

At Crater Lake, the pack-train went into camp, and Churchill, slinging the grip on his back, started the steep climb for the summit. For the first time, on that precipitous wall, he realized how tired he was. He crept and crawled like a crab, burdened by the weight of his limbs. A distinct and painful effort of will was required each time he lifted a foot. An hallucination came to him that he was shod with lead, like a deep-sea diver, and it was all he could do to resist the desire to reach down and feel the lead. As for Bondell's gripsack, it was inconceivable that forty pounds could weigh so much. It pressed him down like a mountain, and he looked back with unbelief to the year before, when he had climbed that same pass with a hundred and fifty pounds on his back. If those loads had weighed a hundred and fifty pounds, then Bondell's grip weighed five hundred.

The first rise of the divide from Crater Lake was across a small glacier. Here was a well-defined trail. But above the glacier, which was also above timber-line, was naught but a chaos of naked rock and enormous boulders. There was no way of seeing the trail in the darkness, and he blundered on, paying thrice the ordinary exertion for all that he accomplished. He won the summit in the thick of howling wind and driving snow, providentially stumbling upon a small, deserted tent, into which he crawled. There he found and bolted some ancient fried potatoes and half a dozen raw eggs.

When the snow ceased and the wind eased down, he began the almost impossible descent. There was no trail, and he stumbled and blundered, often finding himself, at the last moment, on the edge of rocky walls and steep slopes the depth of which he had no way of judging. Part way down, the stars clouded over again, and in the consequent obscurity he slipped and rolled and slid for a hundred feet, landing bruised and bleeding on the bottom of a large shallow hole. From all about him arose the stench of dead horses. The hole was handy to the trail, and the packers had made a practice of tumbling into it their broken and dying animals. The stench overpowered him, making him deadly sick, and as in a nightmare he scrambled out. Half-way up, he recollected Bondell's gripsack. It had fallen into the hole with him; the pack-strap had evidently broken, and he had forgotten it. Back he went into the pestilential charnel-pit, where he crawled around on hands and knees and groped for half an hour. Altogether he encountered and counted seventeen dead horses (and one horse still alive that he shot with his revolver) before he found Bondell's grip. Looking back upon a life that had not been without valour and achievement, he unhesitatingly declared to himself that this return after the grip was the most heroic act he had ever performed. So heroic was it that he was twice on the verge of fainting before he crawled out of the hole.

By the time he had descended to the Scales, the steep pitch of Chilcoot was past, and the way became easier. Not that it was an easy way, however, in the best of places; but it became a really possible trail, along which he could have made good time if he had not been worn out, if he had had light with which to pick his steps, and if it had not been for Bondell's gripsack. To him, in his exhausted condition, it was the last straw. Having barely strength to carry himself along, the additional weight of the grip was sufficient to throw him nearly every time he tripped or stumbled. And when he escaped tripping, branches reached out in the darkness, hooked the grip between his shoulders, and held him back.

His mind was made up that if he missed the *Athenian* it would be the fault of the gripsack. In fact, only two things remained in his consciousness—Bondell's grip and the steamer. He knew only those two things, and they became identified, in a way, with some stern mission upon which he had journeyed and toiled for centuries. He walked and struggled on as in a dream. As part of the dream was his arrival at Sheep Camp. He stumbled into a saloon, slid his shoulders out of the straps, and started to deposit the grip at his feet. But it slipped from his fingers and struck the floor with a heavy thud that was not unnoticed by two men who were just leaving. Churchill drank a glass of whisky, told the barkeeper to call him in ten minutes, and sat down, his feet on the grip, his head on his knees.

So badly did his misused body stiffen, that when he was called it required another ten minutes and a second glass of whisky to unbend his joints and limber up the muscles.

"Hey not that way!" the barkeeper shouted, and then went after him and started him through the darkness toward Canyon City. Some little husk of inner consciousness told Churchill that the direction was right, and, still as in a dream, he took the cañon trail. He did not know what warned him, but after what seemed several centuries of travelling, he sensed danger and drew his revolver. Still in the dream, he saw two men step out and heard them halt him. His revolver went off four times, and he saw the flashes and heard the explosions of their revolvers. Also, he was aware that he had been hit in the thigh. He saw one man go down, and, as the other came for him, he smashed him a straight blow with the heavy revolver full in the face. Then he turned and ran. He came from the dream shortly afterward, to find himself plunging down the trail at a limping lope. His first thought was for the gripsack. It was still on his back. He was convinced that what had happened was a dream till he felt for his revolver and found it gone. Next he became aware of a sharp stinging of his thigh, and after investigating, he found his hand warm with blood. It was a superficial wound, but it was incontestable. He became wider awake, and kept up the lumbering run to Canyon City.

He found a man, with a team of horses and a wagon, who got out of bed and harnessed up for twenty dollars. Churchill crawled in on the wagon-bed and slept, the gripsack still on his back. It was a rough ride, over water-washed boulders down the Dyea Valley; but he roused only when the wagon hit the highest places. Any altitude of his body above the wagon-bed of less than a foot did not faze him. The last mile was smooth going, and he slept soundly.

He came to in the grey dawn, the driver shaking him savagely and howling into his ear that the *Athenian* was gone. Churchill looked blankly at the deserted harbour.

"There's a smoke over at Skaguay," the man said.

Churchill's eyes were too swollen to see that far, but he said: "It's she. Get me a boat."

The driver was obliging and found a skiff, and a man to row it for ten dollars, payment in advance. Churchill paid, and was helped into the skiff. It was beyond him to get in by himself. It was six miles to Skaguay, and he had a blissful thought of sleeping those six miles. But the man did not know how to row, and Churchill took the oars and toiled for a few more centuries. He never knew six longer and more excruciating miles. A snappy little breeze blew up the inlet and held him back. He had a gone feeling at the pit of the stomach, and suffered from faintness and numbness. At his command, the man took the baler and threw salt water into his face.

The *Athenian's* anchor was up-and-down when they came alongside, and Churchill was at the end of his last remnant of strength.

"Stop her! Stop her!" he shouted hoarsely.

"Important message! Stop her!"

Then he dropped his chin on his chest and slept. When half a dozen men started to carry him up the gang-plank, he awoke, reached for the grip, and clung to it like a drowning man.

On deck he became a centre of horror and curiosity. The clothing in which he had left White Horse was represented by a few rags, and he was as frayed as his clothing. He had travelled for fifty-five hours at the top notch of endurance. He had slept six hours in that time, and he was twenty pounds lighter than when he started. Face and hands and body were scratched and bruised, and he could scarcely see. He tried to stand up, but failed, sprawling out on the deck, hanging on to the gripsack, and delivering his message.

"Now, put me to bed," he finished; "I'll eat when I wake up."

They did him honour, carrying him down in his rags and dirt and depositing him and Bondell's grip in the bridal chamber, which was the biggest and most luxurious state-room in the ship. Twice he slept the clock around, and he had bathed and shaved and eaten and was leaning over the rail smoking a cigar when the two hundred pilgrims from White Horse came alongside.

By the time the *Athenian* arrived in Seattle, Churchill had fully recuperated, and he went ashore with Bondell's grip in his hand. He felt proud of that grip. To him it stood for achievement and integrity and trust. "I've delivered the goods," was the way he expressed these various high terms to himself. It was early in the evening, and he went straight to Bondell's home. Louis Bondell was glad to see him, shaking hands with both hands at the same time and dragging him into the house.

"Oh, thanks, old man; it was good of you to bring it out," Bondell said when he received the gripsack.

He tossed it carelessly upon a couch, and Churchill noted with an appreciative eye the rebound of its weight from the springs. Bondell was volleying him with questions.

"How did you make out? How're the boys? What became of Bill Smithers? Is Del Bishop still with Pierce? Did he sell my dogs? How did Sulphur Bottom show up? You're looking fine. What steamer did you come out on?"

To all of which Churchill gave answer, till half an hour had gone by and the first lull in the conversation had arrived.

"Hadn't you better take a look at it?" he suggested, nodding his head at the gripsack.

"Oh, it's all right," Bondell answered. "Did Mitchell's dump turn out as much as he expected?"

"I think you'd better look at it," Churchill insisted. "When I deliver a thing, I want to be satisfied that it's all right. There's always the chance that somebody might have got into it when I was asleep, or something."

"It's nothing important, old man," Bondell answered, with a laugh.

"Nothing important," Churchill echoed in a faint, small voice. Then he spoke with decision: "Louis, what's in that bag? I want to know."

Louis looked at him curiously, then left the room and returned with a bunch of keys. He inserted his hand and drew out a heavy Colt's revolver. Next came out a few boxes of ammunition for the revolver and several boxes of Winchester cartridges.

Churchill took the gripsack and looked into it. Then he turned it upside down and shook it gently.

"The gun's all rusted," Bondell said. "Must have been out in the rain."

"Yes," Churchill answered. "Too bad it got wet. I guess I was a bit careless."

He got up and went outside. Ten minutes later Louis Bondell went out and found him on the steps, sitting down, elbows on knees and chin on hands, gazing steadfastly out into the darkness.

To Build a Fire

D ay had broken cold and grey, exceedingly cold and grey, when the man turned aside from the main Yukon trail and climbed the high earth-bank, where a dim and little-travelled trail led eastward through the fat spruce timberland. It was a steep bank, and he paused for breath at the top, excusing the act to himself by looking at his watch. It was nine o'clock. There was no sun nor hint of sun, though there was not a cloud in the sky. It was a clear day, and yet there seemed an intangible pall over the face of things, a subtle gloom that made the day dark, and that was due to the absence of sun. This fact did not worry the man. He was used to the lack of sun. It had been days since he had seen the sun, and he knew that a few more days must pass before that cheerful orb, due south, would just peep above the sky-line and dip immediately from view.

The man flung a look back along the way he had come. The Yukon lay a mile wide and hidden under three feet of ice. On top of this ice were as many feet of snow. It was all pure white, rolling in gentle undulations where the ice-jams of the freeze-up had formed. North and south, as far as his eye could see, it was unbroken white, save for a dark hair-line that curved and twisted from around the spruce-covered island to the south, and that curved and twisted away into the north, where it disappeared behind another spruce-covered island. This dark hair-line was the trail—the main trail—that led south five hundred miles to the Chilcoot Pass, Dyea, and salt water; and that led north seventy miles to Dawson, and still on to the north a thousand miles to Nulato, and finally to St. Michael on Bering Sea, a thousand miles and half a thousand more.

But all this—the mysterious, far-reaching hairline trail, the absence of sun from the sky, the tremendous cold, and the strangeness and weirdness of it all—made no impression on the man. It was not because he was long used to it. He was a new-comer in the land, a *chechaquo*, and this was his first winter. The trouble with him was that he was without imagination. He was quick and alert in the things of life, but only in the things, and not in the significances. Fifty degrees below zero meant eighty odd degrees of frost. Such fact impressed him as being cold and uncomfortable, and that was all. It did not lead him to meditate upon his frailty as a creature of temperature, and upon man's frailty in general, able only to live within certain narrow limits of heat and cold; and from there on it did not lead him to the conjectural field of immortality and man's place in the universe. Fifty degrees below zero stood for a bite of frost that hurt and that must be guarded against by the use of mittens, ear-flaps, warm moccasins, and thick socks. Fifty degrees below zero was to him just precisely fifty degrees below zero. That there should be anything more to it than that was a thought that never entered his head.

As he turned to go on, he spat speculatively. There was a sharp, explosive crackle that startled him. He spat again. And again, in the air, before it could fall to the snow, the spittle crackled. He knew that at fifty below spittle crackled on the snow, but this spittle had crackled in the air. Undoubtedly it was colder than fifty below—how much colder he did not know. But the temperature did not matter. He was bound for the old claim on the left fork of Henderson Creek, where the boys were already. They had come over across the divide from the Indian Creek country, while he had come the roundabout way to take a look at the possibilities of getting out logs in the spring from the islands in the Yukon. He would be in to camp by six o'clock; a bit after dark, it was true, but the boys would be there, a fire would be going, and a hot supper would be ready. As for lunch, he pressed his hand against the protruding bundle under his jacket. It was also under his shirt, wrapped up in a handkerchief and lying against the naked skin. It was the only way to keep the biscuits from freezing. He smiled agreeably to himself as he thought of those biscuits, each cut open and sopped in bacon grease, and each enclosing a generous slice of fried bacon.

He plunged in among the big spruce trees. The trail was faint. A foot of snow had fallen since the last sled had passed over, and he was glad he was without a sled, travelling light. In fact, he carried nothing but the lunch wrapped in the handkerchief. He was surprised, however, at the cold. It certainly was cold, he concluded, as he rubbed his numbed nose and cheek-bones with his mittened hand. He was a warm-whiskered man, but the hair on his face did not protect the high cheek-bones and the eager nose that thrust itself aggressively into the frosty air.

At the man's heels trotted a dog, a big native husky, the proper wolf-dog, grey-coated and without any visible or temperamental difference from its brother, the wild wolf. The animal was depressed by the tremendous cold. It knew that it was no time for travelling. Its instinct told it a truer tale than was told to the man by the man's judgment. In reality, it was not merely colder than fifty below zero; it was colder than sixty below, than seventy below. It was seventy-five below zero. Since the freezing-point is thirty-two above zero, it meant that one hundred and seven degrees of frost obtained. The dog did not know anything about thermometers. Possibly in its brain there was no sharp consciousness of a condition of very cold such as was in the man's brain. But the brute had its instinct. It experienced a vague but menacing apprehension that subdued it and made it slink along at the man's heels, and that made it question eagerly every unwonted movement of the man as if expecting him to go into camp or to seek shelter somewhere and build a fire. The dog had learned fire, and it wanted fire, or else to burrow under the snow and cuddle its warmth away from the air.

The frozen moisture of its breathing had settled on its fur in a fine powder of frost, and especially were its jowls, muzzle, and eyelashes whitened by its crystalled breath. The man's red beard and moustache were likewise frosted, but more solidly, the deposit taking the form of ice and increasing with every warm, moist breath he exhaled. Also, the man was chewing tobacco, and the muzzle of ice held his lips so rigidly that he was unable to clear his chin when he expelled the juice. The result was that a crystal beard of the colour and solidity of amber was increasing its length on his chin. If he fell down it would shatter itself, like glass, into brittle fragments. But he did not mind the appendage. It was the penalty all tobacco-chewers paid in that country, and he had been out before in two cold snaps. They had not been so cold as this, he knew, but by the spirit thermometer at Sixty Mile he knew they had been registered at fifty below and at fifty-five.

He held on through the level stretch of woods for several miles, crossed a wide flat of nigger-heads, and dropped down a bank to the frozen bed of a small stream. This was Henderson Creek, and he knew he was ten miles from the forks. He looked at his watch. It was ten o'clock. He was making four miles an hour, and he calculated that he would arrive at the forks at half-past twelve. He decided to celebrate that event by eating his lunch there.

The dog dropped in again at his heels, with a tail drooping discouragement, as the man swung along the creek-bed. The furrow of the old sled-trail was plainly visible, but a dozen inches of snow covered the marks of the last runners. In a month no man had come up or down that silent creek. The man held steadily on. He was not much given to thinking, and just then particularly he had nothing to think about save that he would eat lunch at the forks and that at six o'clock he would be in camp with the boys. There was nobody to talk to and, had there been, speech would have been impossible because of the ice-muzzle on his mouth. So he continued monotonously to chew tobacco and to increase the length of his amber beard.

Once in a while the thought reiterated itself that it was very cold and that he had never experienced such cold. As he walked along he rubbed his cheek-bones and nose with the back of his mittened hand. He did this automatically, now and again changing hands. But rub as he would, the instant he stopped his cheek-bones went numb, and the following instant the end of his nose went numb. He was sure to frost his cheeks; he knew that, and experienced a pang of regret that he had not devised a nose-strap of the sort Bud wore in cold snaps. Such a strap passed across the cheeks, as well, and saved them. But it didn't matter much, after all. What were frosted cheeks? A bit painful, that was all; they were never serious.

Empty as the man's mind was of thoughts, he was keenly observant, and he noticed the changes in the creek, the curves and bends and timber-jams, and always he sharply noted where he placed his feet. Once, coming around a bend, he shied abruptly, like a startled horse, curved away from the place where he had been walking, and retreated several paces back along the trail. The creek he knew was frozen clear to the bottom—no creek could contain water in that arctic winter—but he knew also that there were springs that bubbled out from the hillsides and ran along under the snow and on top the ice of the creek. He knew that the coldest snaps never froze these springs, and he knew likewise their danger. They were traps. They hid pools of water under the snow that might be three inches deep, or three feet. Sometimes a skin of ice half an inch thick covered them, and in turn was covered by the snow. Sometimes there were alternate layers of water and ice-skin, so that when one broke through he kept on breaking through for a while, sometimes wetting himself to the waist.

That was why he had shied in such panic. He had felt the give under his feet and heard the crackle of a snow-hidden ice-skin. And to get his feet wet in such a temperature meant trouble and danger. At the very least it meant delay, for he would be forced to stop and build a fire, and under its protection to bare his feet while he dried his socks and moccasins. He stood and studied the creek-bed and its banks, and decided that the flow of water came from the right. He reflected awhile, rubbing his nose and cheeks, then skirted to the left, stepping gingerly and testing the footing for each step. Once clear of the danger, he took a fresh chew of tobacco and swung along at his four-mile gait.

In the course of the next two hours he came upon several similar traps. Usually the snow above the hidden pools had a sunken, candied appearance that advertised the danger. Once again, however, he had a close call; and once, suspecting danger, he compelled the dog to go on in front. The dog did not want to go. It hung back until the man shoved it forward, and then it went quickly across the white, unbroken surface. Suddenly it broke through, floundered to one side, and got away to firmer footing. It had wet its forefeet and legs, and almost immediately the water that clung to it turned to ice. It made quick efforts to lick the ice off its legs, then dropped down in the snow and began to bite out the ice that had formed between the toes. This was a matter of instinct. To permit the ice to remain would mean sore feet. It did not know this. It merely obeyed the mysterious prompting that arose from the deep crypts of its being. But the man knew, having achieved a judgment on the subject, and he removed the mitten from his right hand and helped tear out the ice-particles. He did not expose his fingers more than a minute, and was astonished at the swift numbness that smote them. It certainly was cold. He pulled on the mitten hastily, and beat the hand savagely across his chest.

At twelve o'clock the day was at its brightest. Yet the sun was too far south on its winter journey to clear the horizon. The bulge of the earth intervened between it and Henderson Creek, where the man walked under a clear sky at noon and cast no shadow. At half-past twelve, to the minute, he arrived at the forks of the creek. He was pleased at the speed he had made. If he kept it up, he would certainly be with the boys by six. He unbuttoned his jacket and shirt and drew forth his lunch. The action consumed no more than a quarter of a minute, yet in that brief moment the numbness laid hold of the exposed fingers. He did not put the mitten on, but, instead, struck the fingers a dozen sharp smashes against his leg. Then he sat down on a snow-covered log to eat. The sting that followed upon the striking of his fingers against his leg ceased so quickly that he was startled, he had had no chance to take a bite of biscuit. He struck the fingers repeatedly and returned them to the mitten, baring the other hand for the purpose of eating. He tried to take a mouthful, but the ice-muzzle prevented. He had forgotten to build a fire and thaw out. He chuckled at his foolishness, and as he chuckled he noted the numbness creeping into the exposed fingers. Also, he noted that the stinging which had first come to his toes when he sat down was already passing away. He wondered whether the toes were warm or numbed. He moved them inside the moccasins and decided that they were numbed.

He pulled the mitten on hurriedly and stood up. He was a bit frightened. He stamped up and down until the stinging returned into the feet. It certainly was cold, was his thought. That man from Sulphur Creek had spoken the truth when telling how cold it sometimes got in the country. And he had laughed at him at the time! That showed one must not be too sure of things. There was no mistake about it, it was cold. He strode up and down, stamping his feet and threshing his arms, until reassured by the returning warmth. Then he got out matches and proceeded to make a fire. From the undergrowth, where high water of the previous spring had lodged a supply of seasoned twigs, he got his firewood. Working carefully from a small beginning, he soon had a roaring fire, over which he thawed the ice from his face and in the protection of which he ate his biscuits. For the moment the cold of space was outwitted. The dog took satisfaction in the fire, stretching out close enough for warmth and far enough away to escape being singed.

When the man had finished, he filled his pipe and took his comfortable time over a smoke. Then he pulled on his mittens, settled the ear-flaps of his cap firmly about his ears, and took the creek trail up the left fork. The dog was disappointed and yearned back toward the fire. This man did not know cold. Possibly all the generations of his ancestry had been ignorant of cold, of real cold, of cold one hundred and seven degrees below freezing-point. But the dog knew; all its ancestry knew, and it had inherited the knowledge. And it knew that it was not good to walk abroad in such fearful cold. It was the time to lie snug in a hole in the snow and wait for a curtain of cloud to be drawn across the face of outer space whence this cold came. On the other hand, there was keen intimacy between the dog and the man. The one was the toil-slave of the other, and the only caresses it had ever received were the caresses of the whip-lash and of harsh and menacing throat-sounds that threatened the whip-lash. So the dog made no effort to communicate its apprehension to the man. It was not concerned in the welfare of the man; it was for its own sake that it yearned back toward the fire. But the man whistled, and spoke to it with the sound of whip-lashes, and the dog swung in at the man's heels and followed after.

The man took a chew of tobacco and proceeded to start a new amber beard. Also, his moist breath quickly powdered with white his moustache, eyebrows, and lashes. There did not seem to be so many springs on the left fork of the Henderson, and for half an hour the man saw no signs of any. And then it happened. At a place where there were no signs, where the soft, unbroken snow seemed to advertise solidity beneath, the man broke through. It was not deep. He wetted himself half-way to the knees before he floundered out to the firm crust.

He was angry, and cursed his luck aloud. He had hoped to get into camp with the boys at six o'clock, and this would delay him an hour, for he would have to build a fire and dry out his foot-gear. This was imperative at that low temperature—he knew that much; and he turned aside to the bank, which he climbed. On top, tangled in the underbrush about the trunks of several small spruce trees, was a high-water deposit of dry firewood—sticks and twigs principally, but also larger portions of seasoned branches and fine, dry, last-year's grasses. He threw down several large pieces on top of the snow. This served for a foundation and prevented the young flame from drowning itself in the snow it otherwise would melt. The flame he got by touching a match to a small shred of birch-bark that he took from his pocket. This burned even more readily than paper. Placing it on the foundation, he fed the young flame with wisps of dry grass and with the tiniest dry twigs.

He worked slowly and carefully, keenly aware of his danger. Gradually, as the flame grew stronger, he increased the size of the twigs with which he fed it. He squatted in the snow, pulling the twigs out from their entanglement in the brush and feeding directly to the flame. He knew there must be no failure. When it is seventy-five below zero, a man must not fail in his first attempt to build a fire—that is, if his feet are wet. If his feet are dry, and he fails, he can run along the trail for half a mile and restore his circulation. But the circulation of wet and freezing feet cannot be restored by running when it is seventy-five below. No matter how fast he runs, the wet feet will freeze the harder.

All this the man knew. The old-timer on Sulphur Creek had told him about it the previous fall, and now he was appreciating the advice. Already all sensation had gone out of his feet. To build the fire he had been forced to remove his mittens, and the fingers had quickly gone numb. His pace of four miles an hour had kept his heart pumping blood to the surface of his body and to all the extremities. But the instant he stopped, the action of the pump eased down. The cold of space smote the unprotected tip of the planet, and he, being on that unprotected tip, received the full force of the blow. The blood of his body recoiled before it. The blood was alive, like the dog, and like the dog it wanted to hide away and cover itself up from the fearful cold. So long as he walked four miles an hour, he pumped that blood, willy-nilly, to the surface; but now it ebbed away and sank down into the recesses of his body. The extremities were the first to feel its absence. His wet feet froze the faster, and his exposed fingers numbed the faster, though they had not yet begun to freeze. Nose and cheeks were already freezing, while the skin of all his body chilled as it lost its blood.

But he was safe. Toes and nose and cheeks would be only touched by the frost, for the fire was beginning to burn with strength. He was feeding it with twigs the size of his finger. In another minute he would be able to feed it with branches the size of his wrist, and then he could remove his wet foot-gear, and, while it dried, he could keep his naked feet warm by the fire, rubbing them at first, of course, with snow. The fire was a success. He was safe. He remembered the advice of the old-timer on Sulphur Creek, and smiled. The old-timer had been very serious in laying down the law that no man must travel alone in the Klondike after fifty below. Well, here he was; he had had the accident; he was alone; and he had saved himself. Those old-timers were rather womanish, some of them, he thought. All a man had to do was to keep his head, and he was all right. Any man who was a man could travel alone. But it was surprising, the rapidity with which his cheeks and nose were freezing. And he had not thought his fingers could go lifeless in so short a time. Lifeless they were, for he could scarcely make them move together to grip a twig, and they seemed remote from his body and from him. When he touched a twig, he had to look and see whether or not he had hold of it. The wires were pretty well down between him and his finger-ends.

All of which counted for little. There was the fire, snapping and crackling and promising life with every dancing flame. He started to untie his moccasins. They were coated with ice; the thick German socks were like sheaths of iron half-way to the knees; and the mocassin strings were like rods of steel all twisted and knotted as by some conflagration. For a moment he tugged with his numbed fingers, then, realizing the folly of it, he drew his sheath-knife.

But before he could cut the strings, it happened. It was his own fault or, rather, his mistake. He should not have built the fire under the spruce tree. He should have built it in the open. But it had been easier to pull the twigs from the brush and drop them directly on the fire. Now the tree under which he had done this carried a weight of snow on its boughs. No wind had blown for weeks, and each bough was fully freighted. Each time he had pulled a twig he had communicated a slight agitation to the tree—an imperceptible agitation, so far as he was concerned, but an agitation sufficient to bring about the disaster. High up in the tree one bough capsized its load of snow. This fell on the boughs beneath, capsizing them. This process continued, spreading out and involving the whole tree. It grew like an avalanche, and it descended without warning upon the man and the fire, and the fire was blotted out! Where it had burned was a mantle of fresh and disordered snow.

The man was shocked. It was as though he had just heard his own sentence of death. For a moment he sat and stared at the spot where the fire had been. Then he grew very calm. Perhaps the old-timer on Sulphur Creek was right. If he had only had a trail-mate he would have been in no danger now. The trail-mate could have built the fire. Well, it was up to him to build the fire over again, and this second time there must be no failure. Even if he succeeded, he would most likely lose some toes. His feet must be badly frozen by now, and there would be some time before the second fire was ready.

Such were his thoughts, but he did not sit and think them. He was busy all the time they were passing through his mind, he made a new foundation for a fire, this time in the open; where no treacherous tree could blot it out. Next, he gathered dry grasses and tiny twigs from the high-water flotsam. He could not bring his fingers together to pull them out, but he was able to gather them by the handful. In this way he got many rotten twigs and bits of green moss that were undesirable, but it was the best he could do. He worked methodically, even collecting an armful of the larger branches to be used later when the fire gathered strength. And all the while the dog sat and watched him, a certain yearning wistfulness in its eyes, for it looked upon him as the fire-provider, and the fire was slow in coming.

When all was ready, the man reached in his pocket for a second piece of birch-bark. He knew the bark was there, and, though he could not feel it with his fingers, he could hear its crisp rustling as he fumbled for it. Try as he would, he could not clutch hold of it. And all the time, in his consciousness, was the knowledge that each instant his feet were freezing. This thought tended to put him in a panic, but he fought against it and kept calm. He pulled on his mittens with his teeth, and threshed his arms back and forth, beating his hands with all his might against his sides. He did this sitting down, and he stood up to do it; and all the while the dog sat in the snow, its wolf-brush of a tail curled around warmly over its forefeet, its sharp wolf-ears pricked forward intently as it watched the man. And the man as he beat and threshed with his arms and hands, felt a great surge of envy as he regarded the creature that was warm and secure in its natural covering.

After a time he was aware of the first far-away signals of sensation in his beaten fingers. The faint tingling grew stronger till it evolved into a stinging ache that was excruciating, but which the man hailed with satisfaction. He stripped the mitten from his right hand and fetched forth the birch-bark. The exposed fingers were quickly going numb again. Next he brought out his bunch of sulphur matches. But the tremendous cold had already driven the life out of his fingers. In his effort to separate one match from the others, the whole bunch fell in the snow. He tried to pick it out of the snow, but failed. The dead fingers could neither touch nor clutch. He was very careful. He drove the thought of his freezing feet; and nose, and cheeks, out of his mind, devoting his whole soul to the matches. He watched, using the sense of vision in place of that of touch, and when he saw his fingers on each side the bunch, he closed them—that is, he willed to close them, for the wires were drawn, and the fingers did not obey. He pulled the mitten on the right hand, and beat it fiercely against his knee. Then, with both mittened hands, he scooped the bunch of matches, along with much snow, into his lap. Yet he was no better off.

After some manipulation he managed to get the bunch between the heels of his mittened hands. In this fashion he carried it to his mouth. The ice crackled and snapped when by a violent effort he opened his mouth. He drew the lower jaw in, curled the upper lip out of the way, and scraped the bunch with his upper teeth in order to separate a match. He succeeded in getting one, which he dropped on his lap. He was no better off. He could not pick it up. Then he devised a way. He picked it up in his teeth and scratched it on his leg. Twenty times he scratched before he succeeded in lighting it. As it flamed he held it with his teeth to the birch-bark. But the burning brimstone went up his nostrils and into his lungs, causing him to cough spasmodically. The match fell into the snow and went out.

The old-timer on Sulphur Creek was right, he thought in the moment of controlled despair that ensued: after fifty below, a man should travel with a partner. He beat his hands, but failed in exciting any sensation. Suddenly he bared both hands, removing the mittens with his teeth. He caught the whole bunch between the heels of his hands. His arm-muscles not being frozen enabled him to press the hand-heels tightly against the matches. Then he scratched the bunch along his leg. It flared into flame, seventy sulphur matches at once! There was no wind to blow them out. He kept his head to one side to escape the strangling fumes, and held the blazing bunch to the birch-bark. As he so held it, he became aware of sensation in his hand. His flesh was burning. He could smell it. Deep down below the surface he could feel it. The sensation developed into pain that grew acute. And still he endured it, holding the flame of the matches clumsily to the bark that would not light readily because his own burning hands were in the way, absorbing most of the flame.

At last, when he could endure no more, he jerked his hands apart. The blazing matches fell sizzling into the snow, but the birch-bark was alight. He began laying dry grasses and the tiniest twigs on the flame. He could not pick and choose, for he had to lift the fuel between the heels of his hands. Small pieces of rotten wood and green moss clung to the twigs, and he bit them off as well as he could with his teeth. He cherished the flame carefully and awkwardly. It meant life, and it must not perish. The withdrawal of blood from the surface of his body now made him begin to shiver, and he grew more awkward. A large piece of green moss fell squarely on the little fire. He tried to poke it out with his fingers, but his shivering frame made him poke too far, and he disrupted the nucleus of the little fire, the burning grasses and tiny twigs separating and scattering. He tried to poke them together again, but in spite of the tenseness of the effort, his shivering got away with him, and the twigs were hopelessly scattered. Each twig gushed a puff of smoke and went out. The fire-provider had failed. As he looked apathetically about him, his eyes chanced on the dog, sitting across the ruins of the fire from him, in the snow, making restless, hunching movements, slightly lifting one forefoot and then the other, shifting its weight back and forth on them with wistful eagerness.

The sight of the dog put a wild idea into his head. He remembered the tale of the man, caught in a blizzard, who killed a steer and crawled inside the carcass, and so was saved. He would kill the dog and bury his hands in the warm body until the numbness went out of them. Then he could build another fire. He spoke to the dog, calling it to him; but in his voice was a strange note of fear that frightened the animal, who had never known the man to speak in such way before. Something was the matter, and its suspicious nature sensed danger,—it knew not what danger but somewhere, somehow, in its brain arose an apprehension of the man. It flattened its ears down at the sound of the man's voice, and its restless, hunching movements and the liftings and shiftings of its forefeet became more pronounced but it would not come to the man. He got on his hands and knees and crawled toward the dog. This unusual posture again excited suspicion, and the animal sidled mincingly away.

The man sat up in the snow for a moment and struggled for calmness. Then he pulled on his mittens, by means of his teeth, and got upon his feet. He glanced down at first in order to assure himself that he was really standing up, for the absence of sensation in his feet left him unrelated to the earth. His erect position in itself started to drive the webs of suspicion from the dog's mind; and when he spoke peremptorily, with the sound of whip-lashes in his voice, the dog rendered its customary allegiance and came to him. As it came within reaching distance, the man lost his control. His arms flashed out to the dog, and he experienced genuine surprise when he discovered that his hands could not clutch, that there was neither bend nor feeling in the lingers. He had forgotten for the moment that they were frozen and that they were freezing more and more. All this happened quickly, and before the animal could get away, he encircled its body with his arms. He sat down in the snow, and in this fashion held the dog, while it snarled and whined and struggled.

But it was all he could do, hold its body encircled in his arms and sit there. He realized that he could not kill the dog. There was no way to do it. With his helpless hands he could neither draw nor hold his sheath-knife nor throttle the animal. He released it, and it plunged wildly away, with tail between its legs, and still snarling. It halted forty feet away and surveyed him curiously, with ears sharply pricked forward. The man looked down at his hands in order to locate them, and found them hanging on the ends of his arms. It struck him as curious that one should have to use his eyes in order to find out where his hands were. He began threshing his arms back and forth, beating the mittened hands against his sides. He did this for five minutes, violently, and his heart pumped enough blood up to the surface to put a stop to his shivering.

But no sensation was aroused in the hands. He had an impression that they hung like weights on the ends of his arms, but when he tried to run the impression down, he could not find it.

A certain fear of death, dull and oppressive, came to him. This fear quickly became poignant as he realized that it was no longer a mere matter of freezing his fingers and toes, or of losing his hands and feet, but that it was a matter of life and death with the chances against him. This threw him into a panic, and he turned and ran up the creek-bed along the old, dim trail. The dog joined in behind and kept up with him. He ran blindly, without intention, in fear such as he had never known in his life. Slowly, as he ploughed and floundered through the snow, he began to see things again—the banks of the creek, the old timber-jams, the leafless aspens, and the sky. The running made him feel better. He did not shiver. Maybe, if he ran on, his feet would thaw out; and, anyway, if he ran far enough, he would reach camp and the boys. Without doubt he would lose some fingers and toes and some of his face; but the boys would take care of him, and save the rest of him when he got there. And at the same time there was another thought in his mind that said he would never get to the camp and the boys; that it was too many miles away, that the freezing had too great a start on him, and that he would soon be stiff and dead. This thought he kept in the background and refused to consider. Sometimes it pushed itself forward and demanded to be heard, but he thrust it back and strove to think of other things.

It struck him as curious that he could run at all on feet so frozen that he could not feel them when they struck the earth and took the weight of his body. He seemed to himself to skim along above the surface and to have no connection with the earth. Somewhere he had once seen a winged Mercury, and he wondered if Mercury felt as he felt when skimming over the earth.

His theory of running until he reached camp and the boys had one flaw in it: he lacked the endurance. Several times he stumbled, and finally he tottered, crumpled up, and fell. When he tried to rise, he failed. He must sit and rest, he decided, and next time he would merely walk and keep on going. As he sat and regained his breath, he noted that he was feeling quite warm and comfortable. He was not shivering, and it even seemed that a warm glow had come to his chest and trunk. And yet, when he touched his nose or cheeks, there was no sensation. Running would not thaw them out. Nor would it thaw out his hands and feet. Then the thought came to him that the frozen portions of his body must be extending. He tried to keep this thought down, to forget it, to think of something else; he was aware of the panicky feeling that it caused, and he was afraid of the panic. But the thought asserted itself, and persisted, until it produced a vision of his body totally frozen. This was too much, and he made another wild run along the trail. Once he slowed down to a walk, but the thought of the freezing extending itself made him run again.

And all the time the dog ran with him, at his heels. When he fell down a second time, it curled its tail over its forefeet and sat in front of him facing him curiously eager and intent. The warmth and security of the animal angered him, and he cursed it till it flattened down its ears appeasingly. This time the shivering came more quickly upon the man. He was losing in his battle with the frost. It was creeping into his body from all sides. The thought of it drove him on, but he ran no more than a hundred feet, when he staggered and pitched headlong. It was his last panic. When he had recovered his breath and control, he sat up and entertained in his mind the conception of meeting death with dignity. However, the conception did not come to him in such terms. His idea of it was that he had been making a fool of himself, running around like a chicken with its head cut off—such was the simile that occurred to him. Well, he was bound to freeze anyway, and he might as well take it decently. With this new-found peace of mind came the first glimmerings of drowsiness. A good idea, he thought, to sleep off to death. It was like taking an anæsthetic. Freezing was not so bad as people thought. There were lots worse ways to die.

He pictured the boys finding his body next day. Suddenly he found himself with them, coming along the trail and looking for himself. And, still with them, he came around a turn in the trail and found himself lying in the snow. He did not belong with himself any more, for even then he was out of himself, standing with the boys and looking at himself in the snow. It certainly was cold, was his thought. When he got back to the States he could tell the folks what real cold was. He drifted on from this to a vision of the old-timer on Sulphur Creek. He could see him quite clearly, warm and comfortable, and smoking a pipe.

"You were right, old hoss; you were right," the man mumbled to the old-timer of Sulphur Creek.

Then the man drowsed off into what seemed to him the most comfortable and satisfying sleep he had ever known. The dog sat facing him and waiting. The brief day drew to a close in a long, slow twilight. There were no signs of a fire to be made, and, besides, never in the dog's experience had it known a man to sit like that in the snow and make no fire. As the twilight drew on, its eager yearning for the fire mastered it, and with a great lifting and shifting of forefeet, it whined softly, then flattened its ears down in anticipation of being chidden by the man. But the man remained silent. Later, the dog whined loudly. And still later it crept close to the man and caught the scent of death. This made the animal bristle and back away. A little longer it delayed, howling under the stars that leaped and danced and shone brightly in the cold sky. Then it turned and trotted up the trail in the direction of the camp it knew, where were the other food-providers and fire-providers.

THAT SPOT

I don't think much of Stephen Mackaye any more, though I used to swear by him. I know that in those days I loved him more than my own brother. If ever I meet Stephen Mackaye again, I shall not be responsible for my actions. It passes beyond me that a man with whom I shared food and blanket, and with whom I mushed over the Chilcoot Trail, should turn out the way he did. I always sized Steve up as a square man, a kindly comrade, without an iota of anything vindictive or malicious in his nature. I shall never trust my judgment in men again. Why, I nursed that man through typhoid fever; we starved together on the headwaters of the Stewart; and he saved my life on the Little Salmon. And now, after the years we were together, all I can say of Stephen Mackaye is that he is the meanest man I ever knew.

We started for the Klondike in the fall rush of 1897, and we started too late to get over Chilcoot Pass before the freeze-up. We packed our outfit on our backs part way over, when the snow began to fly, and then we had to buy dogs in order to sled it the rest of the way. That was how we came to get that Spot. Dogs were high, and we paid one hundred and ten dollars for him. He looked worth it. I say *looked*, because he was one of the finest-appearing dogs I ever saw. He weighed sixty pounds, and he had all the lines of a good sled animal. We never could make out his breed. He wasn't husky, nor Malemute, nor Hudson Bay; he looked like all of them and he didn't look like any of them; and on top of it all he had some of the white man's dog in him, for on one side, in the thick of the mixed yellow-brown-red-and-dirty-white that was his prevailing colour, there was a spot of coal-black as big as a water-bucket. That was why we called him Spot.

He was a good looker all right. When he was in condition his muscles stood out in bunches all over him. And he was the strongest-looking brute I ever saw in Alaska, also the most intelligent-looking. To run your eyes over him, you'd think he could outpull three dogs of his own weight. Maybe he could, but I never saw it. His intelligence didn't run that way. He could steal and forage to perfection; he had an instinct that was positively gruesome for divining when work was to be done and for making a sneak accordingly; and for getting lost and not staying lost he was nothing short of inspired. But when it came to work, the way that intelligence dribbled out of him and left him a mere clot of wobbling, stupid jelly would make your heart bleed.

There are times when I think it wasn't stupidity. Maybe, like some men I know, he was too wise to work. I shouldn't wonder if he put it all over us with that intelligence of his. Maybe he figured it all out and decided that a licking now and again and no work was a whole lot better than work all the time and no licking. He was intelligent enough for such a computation. I tell you, I've sat and looked into that dog's eyes till the shivers ran up and down my spine and the marrow crawled like yeast, what of the intelligence I saw shining out. I can't express myself about that intelligence. It is beyond mere words. I saw it, that's all. At times it was like gazing into a human soul, to look into his eyes; and what I saw there frightened me and started all sorts of ideas in my own mind of reincarnation and all the rest. I tell you I sensed something big in that brute's eyes; there was a message there, but I wasn't big enough myself to catch it. Whatever it was (I know I'm making a fool of myself)—whatever it was, it baffled me. I can't give an inkling of what I saw in that brute's eyes; it wasn't light, it wasn't colour; it was something that moved, away back, when the eyes themselves weren't moving. And I guess I didn't see it move either; I only sensed that it moved. It was an expression—that's what it was—and I got an impression of it. No; it was different from a mere expression; it was more than that. I don't know what it was, but it gave me a feeling of kinship just the same. Oh, no, not sentimental kinship. It was, rather, a kinship of equality. Those eyes never pleaded like a deer's eyes. They challenged. No, it wasn't defiance. It was just a calm assumption of equality. And I don't think it was deliberate. My belief is that it was unconscious on his part. It was there because it was there, and it couldn't help shining out. No, I don't mean shine. It didn't shine; it *moved*. I know I'm talking rot, but if you'd looked into that animal's eyes the way I have, you'd understand. Steve was affected the same way I was. Why, I tried to kill that Spot once—he was no good for anything; and I fell down on it. I led him out into the brush, and he came along slow and unwilling. He knew what was going on. I stopped in a likely place, put my foot on the rope, and pulled my big Colt's. And that dog sat down and looked at me. I tell you he didn't plead. He just looked. And I saw all kinds of incomprehensible things moving, yes, *moving*, in those eyes of his. I didn't really see them move; I thought I saw them, for, as I said before, I guess I only sensed them. And I want to tell you right now that it got beyond me. It was like killing a man, a conscious, brave man, who looked calmly into your gun as much as to say, "Who's afraid?"

Then, too, the message seemed so near that, instead of pulling the trigger quick, I stopped to see if I could catch the message. There it was, right before me, glimmering all around in those eyes of his. And then it was too late. I got scared. I was trembly all over, and my stomach generated a nervous palpitation that made me seasick. I just sat down and looked at the dog, and he looked at me, till I thought I was going crazy. Do you want to know what I did? I threw down the gun and ran back to camp with the fear of God in my heart. Steve laughed at me. But I notice that Steve led Spot into the woods, a week later, for the same purpose, and that Steve came back alone, and a little later Spot drifted back, too.

At any rate, Spot wouldn't work. We paid a hundred and ten dollars for him from the bottom of our sack, and he wouldn't work. He wouldn't even tighten the traces. Steve spoke to him the first time we put him in harness, and he sort of shivered, that was all. Not an ounce on the traces. He just stood still and wobbled, like so much jelly. Steve touched him with the whip. He yelped, but not an ounce. Steve touched him again, a bit harder, and he howled—the regular long wolf howl. Then Steve got mad and gave him half a dozen, and I came on the run from the tent.

I told Steve he was brutal with the animal, and we had some words—the first we'd ever had. He threw the whip down in the snow and walked away mad. I picked it up and went to it. That Spot trembled and wobbled and cowered before ever I swung the lash, and with the first bite of it he howled like a lost soul. Next he lay down in the snow. I started the rest of the dogs, and they dragged him along while I threw the whip into him. He rolled over on his back and bumped along, his four legs waving in the air, himself howling as though he was going through a sausage machine. Steve came back and laughed at me, and I apologized for what I'd said.

There was no getting any work out of that Spot; and to make up for it, he was the biggest pig-glutton of a dog I ever saw. On top of that, he was the cleverest thief. There was no circumventing him. Many a breakfast we went without our bacon because Spot had been there first. And it was because of him that we nearly starved to death up the Stewart. He figured out the way to break into our meat-cache, and what he didn't eat, the rest of the team did. But he was impartial. He stole from everybody. He was a restless dog, always very busy snooping around or going somewhere. And there was never a camp within five miles that he didn't raid. The worst of it was that they always came back on us to pay his board bill, which was just, being the law of the land; but it was mighty hard on us, especially that first winter on the Chilcoot, when we were busted, paying for whole hams and sides of bacon that we never ate. He could fight, too, that Spot. He could do everything but work. He never pulled a pound, but he was the boss of the whole team. The way he made those dogs stand around was an education. He bullied them, and there was always one or more of them fresh-marked with his fangs. But he was more than a bully. He wasn't afraid of anything that walked on four legs; and I've seen him march, single-handed into a strange team, without any provocation whatever, and put the *kibosh* on the whole outfit. Did I say he could eat? I caught him eating the whip once. That's straight. He started in at the lash, and when I caught him he was down to the handle, and still going.

But he was a good looker. At the end of the first week we sold him for seventy-five dollars to the Mounted Police. They had experienced dog-drivers, and we knew that by the time he'd covered the six hundred miles to Dawson he'd be a good sled-dog. I say we *knew*, for we were just getting acquainted with that Spot. A little later we were not brash enough to know anything where he was concerned. A week later we woke up in the morning to the dangdest dog-fight we'd ever heard. It was that Spot come back and knocking the team into shape. We ate a pretty depressing breakfast, I can tell you; but cheered up two hours afterward when we sold him to an official courier, bound in to Dawson with government despatches. That Spot was only three days in coming back, and, as usual, celebrated his arrival with a rough house.

We spent the winter and spring, after our own outfit was across the pass, freighting other people's outfits; and we made a fat stake. Also, we made money out of Spot. If we sold him once, we sold him twenty times. He always came back, and no one asked for their money. We didn't want the money. We'd have paid handsomely for any one to take him off our hands for keeps'. We had to get rid of him, and we couldn't give him away, for that would have been suspicious. But he was such a fine looker that we never had any difficulty in selling him. "Unbroke," we'd say, and they'd pay any old price for him. We sold him as low as twenty-five dollars, and once we got a hundred and fifty for him. That particular party returned him in person, refused to take his money back, and the way he abused us was something awful. He said it was cheap at the price to tell us what he thought of us; and we felt he was so justified that we never talked back. But to this day I've never quite regained all the old self-respect that was mine before that man talked to me.

When the ice cleared out of the lakes and river, we put our outfit in a Lake Bennett boat and started for Dawson. We had a good team of dogs, and of course we piled them on top the outfit. That Spot was along—there was no losing him; and a dozen times, the first day, he knocked one or another of the dogs overboard in the course of fighting with them. It was close quarters, and he didn't like being crowded.

"What that dog needs is space," Steve said the second day. "Let's maroon him."

We did, running the boat in at Caribou Crossing for him to jump ashore. Two of the other dogs, good dogs, followed him; and we lost two whole days trying to find them. We never saw those two dogs again; but the quietness and relief we enjoyed made us decide, like the man who refused his hundred and fifty, that it was cheap at the price. For the first time in months Steve and I laughed and whistled and sang. We were as happy as clams. The dark days were over. The nightmare had been lifted. That Spot was gone.

Three weeks later, one morning, Steve and I were standing on the river-bank at Dawson. A small boat was just arriving from Lake Bennett. I saw Steve give a start, and heard him say something that was not nice and that was not under his breath. Then I looked; and there, in the bow of the boat, with ears pricked up, sat Spot. Steve and I sneaked immediately, like beaten curs, like cowards, like absconders from justice. It was this last that the lieutenant of police thought when he saw us sneaking. He surmised that there were law-officers in the boat who were after us. He didn't wait to find out, but kept us in sight, and in the M. & M. saloon got us in a corner. We had a merry time explaining, for we refused to go back to the boat and meet Spot; and finally he held us under guard of another policeman while he went to the boat. After we got clear of him, we started for the cabin, and when we arrived, there was that Spot sitting on the stoop waiting for us. Now how did he know we lived there? There were forty thousand people in Dawson that summer, and how did he *savve* our cabin out of all the cabins? How did he know we were in Dawson, anyway? I leave it to you. But don't forget what I said about his intelligence and that immortal something I have seen glimmering in his eyes.

There was no getting rid of him any more. There were too many people in Dawson who had bought him up on Chilcoot, and the story got around. Half a dozen times we put him on board steamboats going down the Yukon; but he merely went ashore at the first landing and trotted back up the bank. We couldn't sell him, we couldn't kill him (both Steve and I had tried), and nobody else was able to kill him. He bore a charmed life. I've seen him go down in a dogfight on the main street with fifty dogs on top of him, and when they were separated, he'd appear on all his four legs, unharmed, while two of the dogs that had been on top of him would be lying dead.

I saw him steal a chunk of moose-meat from Major Dinwiddie's cache so heavy that he could just keep one jump ahead of Mrs. Dinwiddie's squaw cook, who was after him with an axe. As he went up the hill, after the squaw gave up, Major Dinwiddie himself came out and pumped his Winchester into the landscape. He emptied his magazine twice, and never touched that Spot. Then a policeman came along and arrested him for discharging firearms inside the city limits. Major Dinwiddie paid his fine, and Steve and I paid him for the moose-meat at the rate of a dollar a pound, bones and all. That was what he paid for it. Meat was high that year.

I am only telling what I saw with my own eyes. And now I'll tell you something also. I saw that Spot fall through a water-hole. The ice was three and a half feet thick, and the current sucked him under like a straw. Three hundred yards below was the big water-hole used by the hospital. Spot crawled out of the hospital water-hole, licked off the water, bit out the ice that had formed between his toes, trotted up the bank, and whipped a big Newfoundland belonging to the Gold Commissioner.

In the fall of 1898, Steve and I poled up the Yukon on the last water, bound for Stewart River. We took the dogs along, all except Spot. We figured we'd been feeding him long enough. He'd cost us more time and trouble and money and grub than we'd got by selling him on the Chilcoot—especially grub. So Steve and I tied him down in the cabin and pulled our freight. We camped that night at the mouth of Indian River, and Steve and I were pretty facetious over having shaken him. Steve was a funny cuss, and I was just sitting up in the blankets and laughing when a tornado hit camp. The way that Spot walked into those dogs and gave them what-for was hair-raising. Now how did he get loose? It's up to you. I haven't any theory. And how did he get across the Klondike River? That's another facer. And anyway, how did he know we had gone up the Yukon? You see, we went by water, and he couldn't smell our tracks. Steve and I began to get superstitious about that dog. He got on our nerves, too; and, between you and me, we were just a mite afraid of him.

The freeze-up came on when we were at the mouth of Henderson Creek, and we traded him off for two sacks of flour to an outfit that was bound up White River after copper. Now that whole outfit was lost. Never trace nor hide nor hair of men, dogs, sleds, or anything was ever found. They dropped clean out of sight. It became one of the mysteries of the country. Steve and I plugged away up the Stewart, and six weeks afterward that Spot crawled into camp. He was a perambulating skeleton, and could just drag along; but he got there. And what I want to know is, who told him we were up the Stewart? We could have gone to a thousand other places. How did he know? You tell me, and I'll tell you.

No losing him. At the Mayo he started a row with an Indian dog. The buck who owned the dog took a swing at Spot with an axe, missed him, and killed his own dog. Talk about magic and turning bullets aside—I, for one, consider it a blamed sight harder to turn an axe aside with a big buck at the other end of it. And I saw him do it with my own eyes. That buck didn't want to kill his own dog. You've got to show me.

I told you about Spot breaking into our meat cache. It was nearly the death of us. There wasn't any more meat to be killed, and meat was all we had to live on. The moose had gone back several hundred miles and the Indians with them. There we were. Spring was on, and we had to wait for the river to break. We got pretty thin before we decided to eat the dogs, and we decided to eat Spot first. Do you know what that dog did? He sneaked. Now how did he know our minds were made up to eat him? We sat up nights laying for him, but he never came back, and we ate the other dogs. We ate the whole team.

And now for the sequel. You know what it is when a big river breaks up and a few billion tons of ice go out, jamming and milling and grinding. Just in the thick of it, when the Stewart went out, rumbling and roaring, we sighted Spot out in the middle. He'd got caught as he was trying to cross up above somewhere. Steve and I yelled and shouted and ran up and down the bank, tossing our hats in the air. Sometimes we'd stop and hug each other, we were that boisterous, for we saw Spot's finish. He didn't have a chance in a million. He didn't have any chance at all. After the ice-run, we got into a canoe and paddled down to the Yukon, and down the Yukon to Dawson, stopping to feed up for a week at the cabins at the mouth of Henderson Creek. And as we came in to the bank at Dawson, there sat that Spot, waiting for us, his ears pricked up, his tail wagging, his mouth smiling, extending a hearty welcome to us. Now how did he get out of that ice? How did he know we were coming to Dawson, to the very hour and minute, to be out there on the bank waiting for us?

The more I think of that Spot, the more I am convinced that there are things in this world that go beyond science. On no scientific grounds can that Spot be explained. It's psychic phenomena, or mysticism, or something of that sort, I guess, with a lot of Theosophy thrown in. The Klondike is a good country. I might have been there yet, and become a millionaire, if it hadn't been for Spot. He got on my nerves. I stood him for two years altogether, and then I guess my stamina broke. It was the summer of 1899 when I pulled out. I didn't say anything to Steve. I just sneaked. But I fixed it up all right. I wrote Steve a note, and enclosed a package of "rough-on-rats," telling him what to do with it. I was worn down to skin and bone by that Spot, and I was that nervous that I'd jump and look around when there wasn't anybody within hailing distance. But it was astonishing the way I recuperated when I got quit of him. I got back twenty pounds before I arrived in San Francisco, and by the time I'd crossed the ferry to Oakland I was my old self again, so that even my wife looked in vain for any change in me.

Steve wrote to me once, and his letter seemed irritated. He took it kind of hard because I'd left him with Spot. Also, he said he'd used the "rough-on-rats," per directions, and that there was nothing doing. A year went by. I was back in the office and prospering in all ways— even getting a bit fat. And then Steve arrived. He didn't look me up. I read his name in the steamer list, and wondered why. But I didn't wonder long. I got up one morning and found that Spot chained to the gate-post and holding up the milkman. Steve went north to Seattle, I learned, that very morning. I didn't put on any more weight. My wife made me buy him a collar and tag, and within an hour he showed his gratitude by killing her pet Persian cat. There is no getting rid of that Spot. He will be with me until I die, for he'll never die. My appetite is not so good since he arrived, and my wife says I am looking peaked. Last night that Spot got into Mr. Harvey's hen-house (Harvey is my next-door neighbour) and killed nineteen of his fancy-bred chickens. I shall have to pay for them. My neighbours on the other side quarrelled with my wife and then moved out. Spot was the cause of it. And that is why I am disappointed in Stephen Mackaye. I had no idea he was so mean a man.

Flush of Gold

Lon McFane was a bit grumpy, what of losing his tobacco pouch, or else he might have told me, before we got to it, something about the cabin at Surprise Lake. All day, turn and turn about, we had spelled each other at going to the fore and breaking trail for the dogs. It was heavy snowshoe work, and did not tend to make a man voluble, yet Lon McFane might have found breath enough at noon, when we stopped to boil coffee, with which to tell me. But he didn't. Surprise Lake?—it was Surprise Cabin to me. I had never heard of it before. I confess I was a bit tired. I had been looking for Lon to stop and make camp any time for an hour; but I had too much pride to suggest making camp or to ask him his intentions; and yet he was my man, lured at a handsome wage to mush my dogs for me and to obey my commands. I guess I was a bit grumpy myself. He said nothing, and I was resolved to ask nothing, even if we tramped on all night.

We came upon the cabin abruptly. For a week of trail we had met no one, and, in my mind, there had been little likelihood of meeting any one for a week to come. And yet there it was, right before my eyes, a cabin, with a dim light in the window and smoke curling up from the chimney.

"Why didn't you tell me—" I began, but was interrupted by Lon, who muttered—

"Surprise Lake—it lies up a small feeder half a mile on. It's only a pond."

"Yes, but the cabin—who lives in it?"

"A woman," was the answer, and the next moment Lon had rapped on the door, and a woman's voice bade him enter.

"Have you seen Dave recently?" she asked.

"Nope," Lon answered carelessly. "I've been in the other direction, down Circle City way. Dave's up Dawson way, ain't he?"

The woman nodded, and Lon fell to unharnessing the dogs, while I unlashed the sled and carried the camp outfit into the cabin. The cabin was a large, one-room affair, and the woman was evidently alone in it. She pointed to the stove, where water was already boiling, and Lon set about the preparation of supper, while I opened the fish-bag and fed the dogs. I looked for Lon to introduce us, and was vexed that he did not, for they were evidently old friends.

"You are Lon McFane, aren't you?" I heard her ask him. "Why, I remember you now. The last time I saw you it was on a steamboat, wasn't it? I remember. . ."

Her speech seemed suddenly to be frozen by the spectacle of dread which, I knew, from the tenor I saw mounting in her eyes, must be on her inner vision. To my astonishment, Lon was affected by her words and manner. His face showed desperate, for all his voice sounded hearty and genial, as he said—

"The last time we met was at Dawson, Queen's Jubilee, or Birthday, or something—don't you remember?—the canoe races in the river, and the obstacle races down the main street?"

The terror faded out of her eyes and her whole body relaxed. "Oh, yes, I do remember," she said. "And you won one of the canoe races."

"How's Dave been makin' it lately? Strikin' it as rich as ever, I suppose?" Lon asked, with apparent irrelevance.

She smiled and nodded, and then, noticing that I had unlashed the bed roll, she indicated the end of the cabin where I might spread it. Her own bunk, I noticed, was made up at the opposite end.

"I thought it was Dave coming when I heard your dogs," she said.

After that she said nothing, contenting herself with watching Lon's cooking operations, and listening the while as for the sound of dogs along the trail. I lay back on the blankets and smoked and watched. Here was mystery; I could make that much out, but no more could I make out. Why in the deuce hadn't Lon given me the tip before we arrived? I looked at her face, unnoticed by her, and the longer I looked the harder it was to take my eyes away. It was a wonderfully beautiful face, unearthly, I may say, with a light in it or an expression or something "that was never on land or sea." Fear and terror had completely vanished, and it was a placidly beautiful face—if by "placid" one can characterize that intangible and occult something that I cannot say was a radiance or a light any more than I can say it was an expression.

Abruptly, as if for the first time, she became aware of my presence.

"Have you seen Dave recently?" she asked me. It was on the tip of my tongue to say "Dave who?" when Lon coughed in the smoke that arose from the sizzling bacon. The bacon might have caused that cough, but I took it as a hint and left my question unasked. "No, I haven't," I answered. "I'm new in this part of the country—"

"But you don't mean to say," she interrupted, "that you've never heard of Dave—of Big Dave Walsh?"

"You see," I apologised, "I'm new in the country. I've put in most of my time in the Lower Country, down Nome way."

"Tell him about Dave," she said to Lon.

Lon seemed put out, but he began in that hearty, genial manner that I had noticed before. It seemed a shade too hearty and genial, and it irritated me.

"Oh, Dave is a fine man," he said. "He's a man, every inch of him, and he stands six feet four in his socks. His word is as good as his bond. The man lies who ever says Dave told a lie, and that man will have to fight with me, too, as well—if there's anything left of him when Dave gets done with him. For Dave is a fighter. Oh, yes, he's a scrapper from way back. He got a grizzly with a '38 popgun. He got clawed some, but he knew what he was doin'. He went into the cave on purpose to get that grizzly. 'Fraid of nothing. Free an' easy with his money, or his last shirt an' match when out of money. Why, he drained Surprise Lake here in three weeks an' took out ninety thousand, didn't he?" She flushed and nodded her head proudly. Through his recital she had followed every word with keenest interest. "An' I must say," Lon went on, "that I was disappointed sore on not meeting Dave here to-night."

Lon served supper at one end of the table of whip-sawed spruce, and we fell to eating. A howling of the dogs took the woman to the door. She opened it an inch and listened.

"Where is Dave Walsh?" I asked, in an undertone.

"Dead," Lon answered. "In hell, maybe. I don't know. Shut up."

"But you just said that you expected to meet him here to-night," I challenged.

"Oh, shut up, can't you," was Lon's reply, in the same cautious undertone.

The woman had closed the door and was returning, and I sat and meditated upon the fact that this man who told me to shut up received from me a salary of two hundred and fifty dollars a month and his board.

Lon washed the dishes, while I smoked and watched the woman. She seemed more beautiful than ever—strangely and weirdly beautiful, it is true. After looking at her steadfastly for five minutes, I was compelled to come back to the real world and to glance at Lon McFane. This enabled me to know, without discussion, that the woman, too, was real. At first I had taken her for the wife of Dave Walsh; but if Dave Walsh were dead, as Lon had said, then she could be only his widow.

It was early to bed, for we faced a long day on the morrow; and as Lon crawled in beside me under the blankets, I ventured a question.

"That woman's crazy, isn't she?"

"Crazy as a loon," he answered.

And before I could formulate my next question, Lon McFane, I swear, was off to sleep. He always went to sleep that way—just crawled into the blankets, closed his eyes, and was off, a demure little heavy breathing rising on the air. Lon never snored.

And in the morning it was quick breakfast, feed the dogs, load the sled, and hit the trail. We said good-bye as we pulled out, and the woman stood in the doorway and watched us off. I carried the vision of her unearthly beauty away with me, just under my eyelids, and all I had to do, any time, was to close them and see her again. The way was unbroken, Surprise Lake being far off the travelled trails, and Lon and I took turn about at beating down the feathery snow with our big, webbed shoes so that the dogs could travel. "But you said you expected to meet Dave Walsh at the cabin," trembled on the tip of my tongue a score of times. I did not utter it. I could wait until we knocked off in the middle of the day. And when the middle of the day came, we went right on, for, as Lon explained, there was a camp of moose hunters at the forks of the Teelee, and we could make there by dark. But we didn't make there by dark, for Bright, the lead-dog, broke his shoulder-blade, and we lost an hour over him before we shot him. Then, crossing a timber jam on the frozen bed of the Teelee, the sled suffered a wrenching capsize, and it was a case of make camp and repair the runner. I cooked supper and fed the dogs while Lon made the repairs, and together we got in the night's supply of ice and firewood. Then we sat on our blankets, our moccasins steaming on upended sticks before the fire, and had our evening smoke.

"You didn't know her?" Lon queried suddenly. I shook my head.

"You noticed the colour of her hair and eyes and her complexion, well, that's where she got her name—she was like the first warm glow of a golden sunrise. She was called Flush of Gold. Ever heard of her?"

Somewhere I had a confused and misty remembrance of having heard the name, yet it meant nothing to me. "Flush of Gold," I repeated; "sounds like the name of a dance-house girl." Lon shook his head. "No, she was a good woman, at least in that sense, though she sinned greatly just the same."

"But why do you speak always of her in the past tense, as though she were dead?"

"Because of the darkness on her soul that is the same as the darkness of death. The Flush of Gold that I knew, that Dawson knew, and that Forty Mile knew before that, is dead. That dumb, lunatic creature we saw last night was not Flush of Gold."

"And Dave?" I queried.

"He built that cabin," Lon answered, "He built it for her. . . and for himself. He is dead. She is waiting for him there. She half believes he is not dead. But who can know the whim of a crazed mind? Maybe she wholly believes he is not dead. At any rate, she waits for him there in the cabin he built. Who would rouse the dead? Then who would rouse the living that are dead? Not I, and that is why I let on to expect to meet Dave Walsh there last night. I'll bet a stack that I'd a been more surprised than she if I *had* met him there last night."

"I do not understand," I said. "Begin at the beginning, as a white man should, and tell me the whole tale."

And Lon began. "Victor Chauvet was an old Frenchman—born in the south of France. He came to California in the days of gold. He was a pioneer. He found no gold, but, instead, became a maker of bottled sunshine—in short, a grape-grower and wine-maker. Also, he followed gold excitements. That is what brought him to Alaska in the early days, and over the Chilcoot and down the Yukon long before the Carmack strike. The old town site of Ten Mile was Chauvet's. He carried the first mail into Arctic City. He staked those coal-mines on the Porcupine a dozen years ago. He grubstaked Loftus into the Nippennuck Country. Now it happened that Victor Chauvet was a good Catholic, loving two things in this world, wine and woman. Wine of all kinds he loved, but of woman, only one, and she was the mother of Marie Chauvet."

Here I groaned aloud, having meditated beyond self-control over the fact that I paid this man two hundred and fifty dollars a month.

"What's the matter now?" he demanded.

"Matter?" I complained. "I thought you were telling the story of Flush of Gold. I don't want a biography of your old French wine-bibber."

Lon calmly lighted his pipe, took one good puff, then put the pipe aside. "And you asked me to begin at the beginning," he said.

"Yes," said I; "the beginning."

"And the beginning of Flush of Gold is the old French wine-bibber, for he was the father of Marie Chauvet, and Marie Chauvet was the Flush of Gold. What more do you want? Victor Chauvet never had much luck to speak of. He managed to live, and to get along, and to take good care of Marie, who resembled the one woman he had loved. He took very good care of her. Flush of Gold was the pet name he gave her. Flush of Gold Creek was named after her—Flush of Gold town site, too. The old man was great on town sites, only he never landed them.

"Now, honestly," Lon said, with one of his lightning changes, "you've seen her, what do you think of her—of her looks, I mean? How does she strike your beauty sense?"

"She is remarkably beautiful," I said. "I never saw anything like her in my life. In spite of the fact, last night, that I guessed she was mad, I could not keep my eyes off of her. It wasn't curiosity. It was wonder, sheer wonder, she was so strangely beautiful."

"She was more strangely beautiful before the darkness fell upon her," Lon said softly. "She was truly the Flush of Gold. She turned all men's hearts. . . and heads. She recalls, with an effort, that I once won a canoe race at Dawson—I, who once loved her, and was told by her of her love for me. It was her beauty that made all men love her. She'd 'a' got the apple from Paris, on application, and there wouldn't have been any Trojan War, and to top it off she'd have thrown Paris down. And now she lives in darkness, and she who was always fickle, for the first time is constant—and constant to a shade, to a dead man she does not realize is dead.

"And this is the way it was. You remember what I said last night of Dave Walsh—Big Dave Walsh? He was all that I said, and more, many times more. He came into this country in the late eighties—that's a pioneer for you. He was twenty years old then. He was a young bull. When he was twenty-five he could lift clear of the ground thirteen fifty-pound sacks of flour. At first, each fall of the year, famine drove him out. It was a lone land in those days. No river steamboats, no grub, nothing but salmon bellies and rabbit tracks. But after famine chased him out three years, he said he'd had enough of being chased; and the next year he stayed. He lived on straight meat when he was lucky enough to get it; he ate eleven dogs that winter; but he stayed. And the next winter he stayed, and the next. He never did leave the country again. He was a bull, a great bull. He could kill the strongest man in the country with hard work. He could outpack a Chilcat Indian, he could outpaddle a Stick, and he could travel all day with wet feet when the thermometer registered fifty below zero, and that's going some, I tell you, for vitality. You'd freeze your feet at twenty-five below if you wet them and tried to keep on.

"Dave Walsh was a bull for strength. And yet he was soft and easy-natured. Anybody could do him, the latest short-horn in camp could lie his last dollar out of him. 'But it doesn't worry me,' he had a way of laughing off his softness; 'it doesn't keep me awake nights.' Now don't get the idea that he had no backbone. You remember about the bear he went after with the popgun. When it came to fighting Dave was the blamedest ever. He was the limit, if by that I may describe his unlimitedness when he got into action, he was easy and kind with the weak, but the strong had to give trail when he went by. And he was a man that men liked, which is the finest word of all, a man's man.

"Dave never took part in the big stampede to Dawson when Carmack made the Bonanza strike. You see, Dave was just then over on Mammon Creek strikin' it himself. He discovered Mammon Creek. Cleaned eighty-four thousand up that winter, and opened up the claim so that it promised a couple of hundred thousand for the next winter. Then, summer bein' on and the ground sloshy, he took a trip up the Yukon to Dawson to see what Carmack's strike looked like. And there he saw Flush of Gold. I remember the night. I shall always remember. It was something sudden, and it makes one shiver to think of a strong man with all the strength withered out of him by one glance from the soft eyes of a weak, blond, female creature like Flush of Gold. It was at her dad's cabin, old Victor Chauvet's. Some friend had brought Dave along to talk over town sites on Mammon Creek. But little talking did he do, and what he did was mostly gibberish. I tell you the sight of Flush of Gold had sent Dave clean daffy. Old Victor Chauvet insisted after Dave left that he had been drunk. And so he had. He was drunk, but Flush of Gold was the strong drink that made him so.

"That settled it, that first glimpse he caught of her. He did not start back down the Yukon in a week, as he had intended. He lingered on a month, two months, all summer. And we who had suffered understood, and wondered what the outcome would be. Undoubtedly, in our minds, it seemed that Flush of Gold had met her master. And why not? There was romance sprinkled all over Dave Walsh. He was a Mammon King, he had made the Mammon Creek strike; he was an old sour dough, one of the oldest pioneers in the land—men turned to look at him when he went by, and said to one another in awed undertones, 'There goes Dave Walsh.' And why not? He stood six feet four; he had yellow hair himself that curled on his neck; and he was a bull—a yellow-maned bull just turned thirty-one.

"And Flush of Gold loved him, and, having danced him through a whole summer's courtship, at the end their engagement was made known. The fall of the year was at hand, Dave had to be back for the winter's work on Mammon Creek, and Flush of Gold refused to be married right away. Dave put Dusky Burns in charge of the Mammon Creek claim, and himself lingered on in Dawson. Little use. She wanted her freedom a while longer; she must have it, and she would not marry until next year. And so, on the first ice, Dave Walsh went alone down the Yukon behind his dogs, with the understanding that the marriage would take place when he arrived on the first steamboat of the next year.

"Now Dave was as true as the Pole Star, and she was as false as a magnetic needle in a cargo of loadstone. Dave was as steady and solid as she was fickle and fly-away, and in some way Dave, who never doubted anybody, doubted her. It was the jealousy of his love, perhaps, and maybe it was the message ticked off from her soul to his; but at any rate Dave was worried by fear of her inconstancy. He was afraid to trust her till the next year, he had so to trust her, and he was pretty well beside himself. Some of it I got from old Victor Chauvet afterwards, and from all that I have pieced together I conclude that there was something of a scene before Dave pulled north with his dogs. He stood up before the old Frenchman, with Flush of Gold beside him, and announced that they were plighted to each other. He was very dramatic, with fire in his eyes, old Victor said. He talked something about 'until death do us part'; and old Victor especially remembered that at one place Dave took her by the shoulder with his great paw and almost shook her as he said: 'Even unto death are you mine, and I would rise from the grave to claim you.' Old Victor distinctly remembered those words 'Even unto death are you mine, and I would rise from the grave to claim you.' And he told me afterwards that Flush of Gold was pretty badly frightened, and that he afterwards took Dave to one side privately and told him that that wasn't the way to hold Flush of Gold—that he must humour her and gentle her if he wanted to keep her.

"There is no discussion in my mind but that Flush of Gold was frightened. She was a savage herself in her treatment of men, while men had always treated her as a soft and tender and too utterly-utter something that must not be hurt. She didn't know what harshness was. . . until Dave Walsh, standing his six feet four, a big bull, gripped her and pawed her and assured her that she was his until death, and then some. And besides, in Dawson, that winter, was a music-player—one of those macaroni-eating, greasy-tenor-Eye-talian-dago propositions—and Flush of Gold lost her heart to him. Maybe it was only fascination—I don't know. Sometimes it seems to me that she really did love Dave Walsh. Perhaps it was because he had frightened her with that even-unto-death, rise-from-the-grave stunt of his that she in the end inclined to the dago music-player. But it is all guesswork, and the facts are, sufficient. He wasn't a dago; he was a Russian count—this was straight; and he wasn't a professional piano-player or anything of the sort. He played the violin and the piano, and he sang—sang well—but it was for his own pleasure and for the pleasure of those he sang for. He had money, too—and right here let me say that Flush of Gold never cared a rap for money. She was fickle, but she was never sordid.

"But to be getting along. She was plighted to Dave, and Dave was coming up on the first steamboat to get her—that was the summer of '98, and the first steamboat was to be expected the middle of June. And Flush of Gold was afraid to throw Dave down and face him afterwards. It was all planned suddenly. The Russian music-player, the Count, was her obedient slave. She planned it, I know. I learned as much from old Victor afterwards. The Count took his orders from her, and caught that first steamboat down. It was the *Golden Rocket*. And so did Flush of Gold catch it. And so did I. I was going to Circle City, and I was flabbergasted when I found Flush of Gold on board. I didn't see her name down on the passenger list. She was with the Count fellow all the time, happy and smiling, and I noticed that the Count fellow was down on the list as having his wife along. There it was, state-room, number, and all. The first I knew that he was married, only I didn't see anything of the wife. . . unless Flush of Gold was so counted. I wondered if they'd got married ashore before starting. There'd been talk about them in Dawson, you see, and bets had been laid that the Count fellow had cut Dave out.

"I talked with the purser. He didn't know anything more about it than I did; he didn't know Flush of Gold, anyway, and besides, he was almost rushed to death. You know what a Yukon steamboat is, but you can't guess what the *Golden Rocket* was when it left Dawson that June of 1898. She was a hummer. Being the first steamer out, she carried all the scurvy patients and hospital wrecks. Then she must have carried a couple of millions of Klondike dust and nuggets, to say nothing of a packed and jammed passenger list, deck passengers galore, and bucks and squaws and dogs without end. And she was loaded down to the guards with freight and baggage. There was a mountain of the same on the fore-lower-deck, and each little stop along the way added to it. I saw the box come aboard at Teelee Portage, and I knew it for what it was, though I little guessed the joker that was in it. And they piled it on top of everything else on the fore-lower-deck, and they didn't pile it any too securely either. The mate expected to come back to it again, and then forgot about it. I thought at the time that there was something familiar about the big husky dog that climbed over the baggage and freight and lay down next to the box. And then we passed the *Glendale*, bound up for Dawson. As she saluted us, I thought of Dave on board of her and hurrying to Dawson to Flush of Gold. I turned and looked at her where she stood by the rail. Her eyes were bright, but she looked a bit frightened by the sight of the other steamer, and she was leaning closely to the Count fellow as for protection. She needn't have leaned so safely against him, and I needn't have been so sure of a disappointed Dave Walsh arriving at Dawson. For Dave Walsh wasn't on the *Glendale*. There were a lot of things I didn't know, but was soon to know—for instance, that the pair were not yet married. Inside half an hour preparations for the marriage took place. What of the sick men in the main cabin, and of the crowded condition of the *Golden Rocket*, the likeliest place for the ceremony was found forward, on the lower deck, in an open space next to the rail and gang-plank and shaded by the mountain of freight with the big box on top and the sleeping dog beside it. There was a missionary on board, getting off at Eagle City, which was the next step, so they had to use him quick. That's what they'd planned to do, get married on the boat.

"But I've run ahead of the facts. The reason Dave Walsh wasn't on the *Glendale* was because he was on the *Golden Rocket*. It was this way. After loiterin' in Dawson on account of Flush of Gold, he went down to Mammon Creek on the ice. And there he found Dusky Burns doing so well with the claim, there was no need for him to be around. So he put some grub on the sled, harnessed the dogs, took an Indian along, and pulled out for Surprise Lake. He always had a liking for that section. Maybe you don't know how the creek turned out to be a four-flusher; but the prospects were good at the time, and Dave proceeded to build his cabin and hers. That's the cabin we slept in. After he finished it, he went off on a moose hunt to the forks of the Teelee, takin' the Indian along.

"And this is what happened. Came on a cold snap. The juice went down forty, fifty, sixty below zero. I remember that snap—I was at Forty

Mile; and I remember the very day. At eleven o'clock in the morning the spirit thermometer at the N. A. T. & T. Company's store went down to seventy-five below zero. And that morning, near the forks of the Teelee, Dave Walsh was out after moose with that blessed Indian of his. I got it all from the Indian afterwards—we made a trip over the ice together to Dyea. That morning Mr. Indian broke through the ice and wet himself to the waist. Of course he began to freeze right away. The proper thing was to build a fire. But Dave Walsh was a bull. It was only half a mile to camp, where a fire was already burning. What was the good of building another? He threw Mr. Indian over his shoulder—and ran with him—half a mile—with the thermometer at seventy-five below. You know what that means. Suicide. There's no other name for it. Why, that buck Indian weighed over two hundred himself, and Dave ran half a mile with him. Of course he froze his lungs. Must have frozen them near solid. It was a tomfool trick for any man to do. And anyway, after lingering horribly for several weeks, Dave Walsh died.

"The Indian didn't know what to do with the corpse. Ordinarily he'd have buried him and let it go at that. But he knew that Dave Walsh was a big man, worth lots of money, a *hi-yu skookum* chief. Likewise he'd seen the bodies of other *hi-yu skookums* carted around the country like they were worth something. So he decided to take Dave's body to Forty Mile, which was Dave's headquarters. You know how the ice is on the grass roots in this country—well, the Indian planted Dave under a foot of soil— in short, he put Dave on ice. Dave could have stayed there a thousand years and still been the same old Dave. You understand—just the same as a refrigerator. Then the Indian brings over a whipsaw from the cabin at Surprise Lake and makes lumber enough for the box. Also, waiting for the thaw, he goes out and shoots about ten thousand pounds of moose. This he keeps on ice, too. Came the thaw. The Teelee broke. He built a raft and loaded it with the meat, the big box with Dave inside, and Dave's team of dogs, and away they went down the Teelee.

"The raft got caught on a timber jam and hung up two days. It was scorching hot weather, and Mr. Indian nearly lost his moose meat. So when he got to Teelee Portage he figured a steamboat would get to Forty Mile quicker than his raft. He transferred his cargo, and there you are, fore-lower deck of the *Golden Rocket*, Flush of Gold being married, and Dave Walsh in his big box casting the shade for her. And there's one thing I clean forgot. No wonder I thought the husky dog that came aboard at Teelee Portage was familiar. It was Pee-lat, Dave

Walsh's lead-dog and favourite—a terrible fighter, too. He was lying down beside the box.

"Flush of Gold caught sight of me, called me over, shook hands with me, and introduced me to the Count. She was beautiful. I was as mad for her then as ever. She smiled into my eyes and said I must sign as one of the witnesses. And there was no refusing her. She was ever a child, cruel as children are cruel. Also, she told me she was in possession of the only two bottles of champagne in Dawson—or that had been in Dawson the night before; and before I knew it I was scheduled to drink her and the Count's health. Everybody crowded round, the captain of the steamboat, very prominent, trying to ring in on the wine, I guess. It was a funny wedding. On the upper deck the hospital wrecks, with various feet in the grave, gathered and looked down to see. There were Indians all jammed in the circle, too, big bucks, and their squaws and kids, to say nothing of about twenty-five snarling wolf-dogs. The missionary lined the two of them up and started in with the service. And just then a dog-fight started, high up on the pile of freight—Pee-lat lying beside the big box, and a white-haired brute belonging to one of the Indians. The fight wasn't explosive at all. The brutes just snarled at each other from a distance—tapping at each other long-distance, you know, saying dast and dassent, dast and dassent. The noise was rather disturbing, but you could hear the missionary's voice above it.

"There was no particularly easy way of getting at the two dogs, except from the other side of the pile. But nobody was on that side—everybody watching the ceremony, you see. Even then everything might have been all right if the captain hadn't thrown a club at the dogs. That was what precipitated everything. As I say, if the captain hadn't thrown that club, nothing might have happened.

"The missionary had just reached the point where he was saying 'In sickness and in health,' and 'Till death us do part.' And just then the captain threw the club. I saw the whole thing. It landed on Pee-lat, and at that instant the white brute jumped him. The club caused it. Their two bodies struck the box, and it began to slide, its lower end tilting down. It was a long oblong box, and it slid down slowly until it reached the perpendicular, when it came down on the run. The onlookers on that side the circle had time to get out from under. Flush of Gold and the Count, on the opposite side of the circle, were facing the box; the missionary had his back to it. The box must have fallen ten feet straight up and down, and it hit end on.

"Now mind you, not one of us knew that Dave Walsh was dead. We thought he was on the *Glendale*, bound for Dawson. The missionary had edged off to one side, and so Flush of Gold faced the box when it struck. It was like in a play. It couldn't have been better planned. It struck on end, and on the right end; the whole front of the box came off; and out swept Dave Walsh on his feet, partly wrapped in a blanket, his yellow hair flying and showing bright in the sun. Right out of the box, on his feet, he swept upon Flush of Gold. She didn't know he was dead, but it was unmistakable, after hanging up two days on a timber jam, that he was rising all right from the dead to claim her. Possibly that is what she thought. At any rate, the sight froze her. She couldn't move. She just sort of wilted and watched Dave Walsh coming for her! And he got her. It looked almost as though he threw his arms around her, but whether or not this happened, down to the deck they went together. We had to drag Dave Walsh's body clear before we could get hold of her. She was in a faint, but it would have been just as well if she had never come out of that faint; for when she did, she fell to screaming the way insane people do. She kept it up for hours, till she was exhausted. Oh, yes, she recovered. You saw her last night, and know how much recovered she is. She is not violent, it is true, but she lives in darkness. She believes that she is waiting for Dave Walsh, and so she waits in the cabin he built for her. She is no longer fickle. It is nine years now that she has been faithful to Dave Walsh, and the outlook is that she'll be faithful to him to the end."

Lon McFane pulled down the top of the blankets and prepared to crawl in.

"We have her grub hauled to her each year," he added, "and in general keep an eye on her. Last night was the first time she ever recognized me, though."

"Who are the we?" I asked.

"Oh," was the answer, "the Count and old Victor Chauvet and me. Do you know, I think the Count is the one to be really sorry for. Dave Walsh never did know that she was false to him. And she does not suffer. Her darkness is merciful to her."

I lay silently under the blankets for the space of a minute.

"Is the Count still in the country?" I asked.

But there was a gentle sound of heavy breathing, and I knew Lon McFane was asleep.

THE PASSING OF MARCUS O'BRIEN

I t is the judgment of this court that you vamose the camp. . . in the customary way, sir, in the customary way."

Judge Marcus O'Brien was absent-minded, and Mucluc Charley nudged him in the ribs. Marcus O'Brien cleared his throat and went on—

"Weighing the gravity of the offence, sir, and the extenuating circumstances, it is the opinion of this court, and its verdict, that you be outfitted with three days' grub. That will do, I think."

Arizona Jack cast a bleak glance out over the Yukon. It was a swollen, chocolate flood, running a mile wide and nobody knew how deep. The earth-bank on which he stood was ordinarily a dozen feet above the water, but the river was now growling at the top of the bank, devouring, instant by instant, tiny portions of the top-standing soil. These portions went into the gaping mouths of the endless army of brown swirls and vanished away. Several inches more, and Red Cow would be flooded.

"It won't do," Arizona Jack said bitterly. "Three days' grub ain't enough."

"There was Manchester," Marcus O'Brien replied gravely. "He didn't get any grub."

"And they found his remains grounded on the Lower River an' half eaten by huskies," was Arizona Jack's retort. "And his killin' was without provocation. Joe Deeves never did nothin', never warbled once, an' jes' because his stomach was out of order, Manchester ups an' plugs him. You ain't givin' me a square deal, O'Brien, I tell you that straight. Give me a week's grub, and I play even to win out. Three days' grub, an' I cash in."

"What for did you kill Ferguson?" O'Brien demanded. "I haven't any patience for these unprovoked killings. And they've got to stop. Red Cow's none so populous. It's a good camp, and there never used to be any killings. Now they're epidemic. I'm sorry for you, Jack, but you've got to be made an example of. Ferguson didn't provoke enough for a killing."

"Provoke!" Arizona Jack snorted. "I tell you, O'Brien, you don't savve. You ain't got no artistic sensibilities. What for did I kill Ferguson? What for did Ferguson sing 'Then I wisht I was a little bird'? That's what I want to know. Answer me that. What for did he sing 'little bird, little bird'? One little bird was enough. I could a-stood one little bird. But no, he must sing two little birds. I gave 'm a chanst. I went to him almighty polite and requested him kindly to discard one little bird. I pleaded with him. There was witnesses that testified to that.

"An' Ferguson was no jay-throated songster," some one spoke up from the crowd.

O'Brien betrayed indecision.

"Ain't a man got a right to his artistic feelin's?" Arizona Jack demanded. "I gave Ferguson warnin'. It was violatin' my own nature to go on listening to his little birds. Why, there's music sharps that fine-strung an' keyed-up they'd kill for heaps less'n I did. I'm willin' to pay for havin' artistic feelin's. I can take my medicine an' lick the spoon, but three days' grub is drawin' it a shade fine, that's all, an' I hereby register my kick. Go on with the funeral."

O'Brien was still wavering. He glanced inquiringly at Mucluc Charley.

"I should say, Judge, that three days' grub was a mite severe," the latter suggested; "but you're runnin' the show. When we elected you judge of this here trial court, we agreed to abide by your decisions, an' we've done it, too, b'gosh, an' we're goin' to keep on doin' it."

"Mebbe I've been a trifle harsh, Jack," O'Brien said apologetically—"I'm that worked up over those killings; an' I'm willing to make it a week's grub." He cleared his throat magisterially and looked briskly about him. "And now we might as well get along and finish up the business. The boat's ready. You go and get the grub, Leclaire. We'll settle for it afterward."

Arizona Jack looked grateful, and, muttering something about "damned little birds," stepped aboard the open boat that rubbed restlessly against the bank. It was a large skiff, built of rough pine planks that had been sawed by hand from the standing timber of Lake Linderman, a few hundred miles above, at the foot of Chilcoot. In the boat were a pair of oars and Arizona Jack's blankets. Leclaire brought the grub, tied up in a flour-sack, and put it on board. As he did so, he whispered—"I gave you good measure, Jack. You done it with provocation."

"Cast her off!" Arizona Jack cried.

Somebody untied the painter and threw it in. The current gripped the boat and whirled it away. The murderer did not bother with the oars, contenting himself with sitting in the stern-sheets and rolling a cigarette. Completing it, he struck a match and lighted up. Those that watched on the bank could see the tiny puffs of smoke. They remained on the bank till the boat swung out of sight around the bend half a mile below. Justice had been done.

The denizens of Red Cow imposed the law and executed sentences without the delays that mark the softness of civilization. There was no law on the Yukon save what they made for themselves. They were compelled to make it for themselves. It was in an early day that Red Cow flourished on the Yukon—1887—and the Klondike and its populous stampedes lay in the unguessed future. The men of Red Cow did not even know whether their camp was situated in Alaska or in the North-west Territory, whether they drew breath under the stars and stripes or under the British flag. No surveyor had ever happened along to give them their latitude and longitude. Red Cow was situated somewhere along the Yukon, and that was sufficient for them. So far as flags were concerned, they were beyond all jurisdiction. So far as the law was concerned, they were in No-Man's land.

They made their own law, and it was very simple. The Yukon executed their decrees. Some two thousand miles below Red Cow the Yukon flowed into Bering Sea through a delta a hundred miles wide. Every mile of those two thousand miles was savage wilderness. It was true, where the Porcupine flowed into the Yukon inside the Arctic Circle there was a Hudson Bay Company trading post. But that was many hundreds of miles away. Also, it was rumoured that many hundreds of miles farther on there were missions. This last, however, was merely rumour; the men of Red Cow had never been there. They had entered the lone land by way of Chilcoot and the head-waters of the Yukon.

The men of Red Cow ignored all minor offences. To be drunk and disorderly and to use vulgar language were looked upon as natural and inalienable rights. The men of Red Cow were individualists, and recognized as sacred but two things, property and life. There were no women present to complicate their simple morality. There were only three log-cabins in Red Cow—the majority of the population of forty men living in tents or brush shacks; and there was no jail in which to confine malefactors, while the inhabitants were too busy digging gold or seeking gold to take a day off and build a jail. Besides, the paramount question of grub negatived such a procedure. Wherefore, when a man violated the rights of property or life, he was thrown into an open boat and started down the Yukon. The quantity of grub he received was proportioned to the gravity of the offence. Thus, a common thief might get as much as two weeks' grub; an uncommon thief might get no more than half of that. A murderer got no grub at all. A man found guilty of manslaughter would receive grub for from three days to a week. And Marcus O'Brien had been elected judge, and it was he who apportioned the grub. A man who broke the law took his chances. The Yukon swept him away, and he might or might not win to Bering Sea. A few days' grub gave him a fighting chance. No grub meant practically capital punishment, though there was a slim chance, all depending on the season of the year.

Having disposed of Arizona Jack and watched him out of sight, the population turned from the bank and went to work on its claims—all except Curly Jim, who ran the one faro layout in all the Northland and who speculated in prospect-holes on the sides. Two things happened that day that were momentous. In the late morning Marcus O'Brien struck it. He washed out a dollar, a dollar and a half, and two dollars, from three successive pans. He had found the streak. Curly Jim looked into the hole, washed a few pans himself, and offered O'Brien ten thousand dollars for all rights—five thousand in dust, and, in lieu of the other five thousand, a half interest in his faro layout. O'Brien refused the offer. He was there to make money out of the earth, he declared with heat, and not out of his fellow-men. And anyway, he didn't like faro. Besides, he appraised his strike at a whole lot more than ten thousand.

The second event of moment occurred in the afternoon, when Siskiyou Pearly ran his boat into the bank and tied up. He was fresh from the Outside, and had in his possession a four-months-old newspaper. Furthermore, he had half a dozen barrels of whisky, all consigned to Curly Jim. The men of Red Cow quit work. They sampled the whisky— at a dollar a drink, weighed out on Curly's scales; and they discussed the news. And all would have been well, had not Curly Jim conceived a nefarious scheme, which was, namely, first to get Marcus O'Brien drunk, and next, to buy his mine from him.

The first half of the scheme worked beautifully. It began in the early evening, and by nine o'clock O'Brien had reached the singing stage. He clung with one arm around Curly Jim's neck, and even essayed the late lamented Ferguson's song about the little birds. He considered he was quite safe in this, what of the fact that the only man in camp with artistic feelings was even then speeding down the Yukon on the breast of a five-mile current.

But the second half of the scheme failed to connect. No matter how much whisky was poured down his neck, O'Brien could not be brought to realize that it was his bounden and friendly duty to sell his claim. He hesitated, it is true, and trembled now and again on the verge of giving in. Inside his muddled head, however, he was chuckling to himself. He was up to Curly Jim's game, and liked the hands that were being dealt him. The whisky was good. It came out of one special barrel, and was about a dozen times better than that in the other five barrels.

Siskiyou Pearly was dispensing drinks in the bar-room to the remainder of the population of Red Cow, while O'Brien and Curly had out their business orgy in the kitchen. But there was nothing small about O'Brien. He went into the bar-room and returned with Mucluc Charley and Percy Leclaire.

"Business 'sociates of mine, business 'sociates," he announced, with a broad wink to them and a guileless grin to Curly. "Always trust their judgment, always trust 'em. They're all right. Give 'em some fire-water, Curly, an' le's talk it over."

This was ringing in; but Curly Jim, making a swift revaluation of the claim, and remembering that the last pan he washed had turned out seven dollars, decided that it was worth the extra whisky, even if it was selling in the other room at a dollar a drink.

"I'm not likely to consider," O'Brien was hiccoughing to his two friends in the course of explaining to them the question at issue. "Who? Me?—sell for ten thousand dollars! No indeed. I'll dig the gold myself, an' then I'm goin' down to God's country—Southern California—that's the place for me to end my declinin' days—an' then I'll start. . . as I said before, then I'll start. . . what did I say I was goin' to start?"

"Ostrich farm," Mucluc Charley volunteered.

"Sure, just what I'm goin' to start." O'Brien abruptly steadied himself and looked with awe at Mucluc Charley. "How did you know? Never said so. Jes' thought I said so. You're a min' reader, Charley. Le's have another."

Curly Jim filled the glasses and had the pleasure of seeing four dollars' worth of whisky disappear, one dollar's worth of which he punished himself—O'Brien insisted that he should drink as frequently as his guests.

"Better take the money now," Leclaire argued. "Take you two years to dig it out the hole, an' all that time you might be hatchin' teeny little baby ostriches an' pulling feathers out the big ones."

O'Brien considered the proposition and nodded approval. Curly Jim looked gratefully at Leclaire and refilled the glasses.

"Hold on there!" spluttered Mucluc Charley, whose tongue was beginning to wag loosely and trip over itself. "As your father confessor— there I go—as your brother—O hell!" He paused and collected himself for another start. "As your frien'—business frien', I should say, I would suggest, rather—I would take the liberty, as it was, to mention—I mean, suggest, that there may be more ostriches. . . O hell!" He downed another glass, and went on more carefully. "What I'm drivin' at is. . . what am I drivin' at?" He smote the side of his head sharply half a dozen times with the heel of his palm to shake up his ideas. "I got it!" he cried jubilantly. "Supposen there's slathers more'n ten thousand dollars in that hole!"

O'Brien, who apparently was all ready to close the bargain, switched about.

"Great!" he cried. "Splen'd idea. Never thought of it all by myself." He took Mucluc Charley warmly by the hand. "Good frien'! Good 's'ciate!" He turned belligerently on Curly Jim. "Maybe hundred thousand dollars in that hole. You wouldn't rob your old frien', would you, Curly? Course you wouldn't. I know you—better'n yourself, better'n yourself. Le's have another: We're good frien's, all of us, I say, all of us."

And so it went, and so went the whisky, and so went Curly Jim's hopes up and down. Now Leclaire argued in favour of immediate sale, and almost won the reluctant O'Brien over, only to lose him to the more brilliant counter-argument of Mucluc Charley. And again, it was Mucluc Charley who presented convincing reasons for the sale and Percy Leclaire who held stubbornly back. A little later it was O'Brien himself who insisted on selling, while both friends, with tears and curses, strove to dissuade him. The more whiskey they downed, the more fertile of imagination they became. For one sober pro or con they found a score of drunken ones; and they convinced one another so readily that they were perpetually changing sides in the argument.

The time came when both Mucluc Charley and Leclaire were firmly set upon the sale, and they gleefully obliterated O'Brien's objections as fast as he entered them. O'Brien grew desperate. He exhausted his last argument and sat speechless. He looked pleadingly at the friends who had deserted him. He kicked Mucluc Charley's shins under the table, but that graceless hero immediately unfolded a new and most logical reason for the sale. Curly Jim got pen and ink and paper and wrote out the bill of sale. O'Brien sat with pen poised in hand.

"Le's have one more," he pleaded. "One more before I sign away a hundred thousan' dollars."

Curly Jim filled the glasses triumphantly. O'Brien downed his drink and bent forward with wobbling pen to affix his signature. Before he had made more than a blot, he suddenly started up, impelled by the impact of an idea colliding with his consciousness. He stood upon his feet and swayed back and forth before them, reflecting in his startled eyes the thought process that was taking place behind. Then he reached his conclusion. A benevolent radiance suffused his countenance. He turned to the faro dealer, took his hand, and spoke solemnly.

"Curly, you're my frien'. There's my han'. Shake. Ol' man, I won't do it. Won't sell. Won't rob a frien'. No son-of-a-gun will ever have chance to say Marcus O'Brien robbed frien' cause frien' was drunk. You're drunk, Curly, an' I won't rob you. Jes' had thought—never thought it before—don't know what the matter 'ith me, but never thought it before. Suppose, jes' suppose, Curly, my ol' frien', jes' suppose there ain't ten thousan' in whole damn claim. You'd be robbed. No, sir; won't do it. Marcus O'Brien makes money out of the groun', not out of his frien's."

Percy Leclaire and Mucluc Charley drowned the faro dealer's objections in applause for so noble a sentiment. They fell upon O'Brien from either side, their arms lovingly about his neck, their mouths so full of words they could not hear Curly's offer to insert a clause in the document to the effect that if there weren't ten thousand in the claim he would be given back the difference between yield and purchase price. The longer they talked the more maudlin and the more noble the discussion became. All sordid motives were banished. They were a trio of philanthropists striving to save Curly Jim from himself and his own philanthropy. They insisted that he was a philanthropist. They refused to accept for a moment that there could be found one ignoble thought in all the world. They crawled and climbed and scrambled over high ethical plateaux and ranges, or drowned themselves in metaphysical seas of sentimentality.

Curly Jim sweated and fumed and poured out the whisky. He found himself with a score of arguments on his hands, not one of which had anything to do with the gold-mine he wanted to buy. The longer they talked the farther away they got from that gold-mine, and at two in the morning Curly Jim acknowledged himself beaten. One by one he led his helpless guests across the kitchen floor and thrust them outside. O'Brien came last, and the three, with arms locked for mutual aid, titubated gravely on the stoop.

"Good business man, Curly," O'Brien was saying. "Must say like your style—fine an' generous, free-handed hospital. . . hospital. . . hospitality. Credit to you. Nothin' base 'n graspin' in your make-up. As I was sayin'—"

But just then the faro dealer slammed the door.

The three laughed happily on the stoop. They laughed for a long time. Then Mucluc Charley essayed speech.

"Funny—laughed so hard—ain't what I want to say. My idea is. . . what wash it? Oh, got it! Funny how ideas slip. Elusive idea—chasin' elusive idea—great sport. Ever chase rabbits, Percy, my frien'? I had dog—great rabbit dog. Whash 'is name? Don't know name—never had no name—forget name—elusive name—chasin' elusive name—no, idea—elusive idea, but got it—what I want to say was—O hell!"

Thereafter there was silence for a long time. O'Brien slipped from their arms to a sitting posture on the stoop, where he slept gently. Mucluc Charley chased the elusive idea through all the nooks and crannies of his drowning consciousness. Leclaire hung fascinated upon the delayed utterance. Suddenly the other's hand smote him on the back.

"Got it!" Mucluc Charley cried in stentorian tones.

The shock of the jolt broke the continuity of Leclaire's mental process.

"How much to the pan?" he demanded.

"Pan nothin'!" Mucluc Charley was angry. "Idea—got it—got leg-hold—ran it down."

Leclaire's face took on a rapt, admiring expression, and again he hung upon the other's lips.

". . . O hell!" said Mucluc Charley.

At this moment the kitchen door opened for an instant, and Curly Jim shouted, "Go home!"

"Funny," said Mucluc Charley. "Shame idea—very shame as mine. Le's go home."

They gathered O'Brien up between them and started. Mucluc Charley began aloud the pursuit of another idea. Leclaire followed the pursuit with enthusiasm. But O'Brien did not follow it. He neither heard, nor saw, nor knew anything. He was a mere wobbling automaton, supported affectionately and precariously by his two business associates.

They took the path down by the bank of the Yukon. Home did not lie that way, but the elusive idea did. Mucluc Charley giggled over the idea that he could not catch for the edification of Leclaire. They came to where Siskiyou Pearly's boat lay moored to the bank. The rope with which it was tied ran across the path to a pine stump. They tripped over it and went down, O'Brien underneath. A faint flash of consciousness lighted his brain. He felt the impact of bodies upon his and struck out madly for a moment with his fists. Then he went to sleep again. His gentle snore arose on the air, and Mucluc Charley began to giggle.

"New idea," he volunteered, "brand new idea. Jes' caught it—no trouble at all. Came right up an' I patted it on the head. It's mine. 'Brien's drunk—beashly drunk. Shame—damn shame—learn'm lesshon. Trash Pearly's boat. Put 'Brien in Pearly's boat. Casht off—let her go down Yukon. 'Brien wake up in mornin'. Current too strong—can't row boat 'gainst current—mush walk back. Come back madder 'n hatter. You an' me headin' for tall timber. Learn 'm lesshon jes' shame, learn 'm lesshon."

Siskiyou Pearly's boat was empty, save for a pair of oars. Its gunwale rubbed against the bank alongside of O'Brien. They rolled him over into it. Mucluc Charley cast off the painter, and Leclaire shoved the boat out into the current. Then, exhausted by their labours, they lay down on the bank and slept.

Next morning all Red Cow knew of the joke that had been played on Marcus O'Brien. There were some tall bets as to what would happen to the two perpetrators when the victim arrived back. In the afternoon a lookout was set, so that they would know when he was sighted. Everybody wanted to see him come in. But he didn't come, though they sat up till midnight. Nor did he come next day, nor the next. Red Cow never saw Marcus O'Brien again, and though many conjectures were entertained, no certain clue was ever gained to dispel the mystery of his passing.

ONLY MARCUS O'BRIEN KNEW, AND he never came back to tell. He awoke next morning in torment. His stomach had been calcined by the inordinate quantity of whisky he had drunk, and was a dry and raging furnace. His head ached all over, inside and out; and, worse than that, was the pain in his face. For six hours countless thousands of mosquitoes had fed upon him, and their ungrateful poison had swollen his face tremendously. It was only by a severe exertion of will that he was able to open narrow slits in his face through which he could peer. He happened to move his hands, and they hurt. He squinted at them, but failed to recognize them, so puffed were they by the mosquito virus.

He was lost, or rather, his identity was lost to him. There was nothing familiar about him, which, by association of ideas, would cause to rise in his consciousness the continuity of his existence. He was divorced utterly from his past, for there was nothing about him to resurrect in his consciousness a memory of that past. Besides, he was so sick and miserable that he lacked energy and inclination to seek after who and what he was.

It was not until he discovered a crook in a little finger, caused by an unset breakage of years before, that he knew himself to be Marcus O'Brien. On the instant his past rushed into his consciousness. When he discovered a blood-blister under a thumb-nail, which he had received the previous week, his self-identification became doubly sure, and he knew that those unfamiliar hands belonged to Marcus O'Brien, or, just as much to the point, that Marcus O'Brien belonged to the hands. His first thought was that he was ill—that he had had river fever. It hurt him so much to open his eyes that he kept them closed. A small floating branch struck the boat a sharp rap. He thought it was some one knocking on the cabin door, and said, "Come in." He waited for a while, and then said testily, "Stay out, then, damn you." But just the same he wished they would come in and tell him about his illness.

But as he lay there, the past night began to reconstruct itself in his brain. He hadn't been sick at all, was his thought; he had merely been drunk, and it was time for him to get up and go to work. Work suggested his mine, and he remembered that he had refused ten thousand dollars for it. He sat up abruptly and squeezed open his eyes. He saw himself in a boat, floating on the swollen brown flood of the Yukon. The spruce-covered shores and islands were unfamiliar. He was stunned for a time. He couldn't make it out. He could remember the last night's orgy, but there was no connection between that and his present situation.

He closed his eyes and held his aching head in his hands. What had happened? Slowly the dreadful thought arose in his mind. He fought against it, strove to drive it away, but it persisted: he had killed somebody. That alone could explain why he was in an open boat drifting down the Yukon. The law of Red Cow that he had so long administered had now been administered to him. He had killed some one and been set adrift. But whom? He racked his aching brain for the answer, but all that came was a vague memory of bodies falling upon him and of striking out at them. Who were they? Maybe he had killed more than one. He reached to his belt. The knife was missing from its sheath. He had done it with that undoubtedly. But there must have been some reason for the killing. He opened his eyes and in a panic began to search about the boat. There was no grub, not an ounce of grub. He sat down with a groan. He had killed without provocation. The extreme rigour of the law had been visited upon him.

For half an hour he remained motionless, holding his aching head and trying to think. Then he cooled his stomach with a drink of water from overside and felt better. He stood up, and alone on the wide-stretching Yukon, with naught but the primeval wilderness to hear, he cursed strong drink. After that he tied up to a huge floating pine that was deeper sunk in the current than the boat and that consequently drifted faster. He washed his face and hands, sat down in the stern-sheets, and did some more thinking. It was late in June. It was two thousand miles to Bering Sea. The boat was averaging five miles an hour. There was no darkness in such high latitudes at that time of the year, and he could run the river every hour of the twenty-four. This would mean, daily, a hundred and twenty miles. Strike out the twenty for accidents, and there remained a hundred miles a day. In twenty days he would reach Bering Sea. And this would involve no expenditure of energy; the river did the work. He could lie down in the bottom of the boat and husband his strength.

For two days he ate nothing. Then, drifting into the Yukon Flats, he went ashore on the low-lying islands and gathered the eggs of wild geese and ducks. He had no matches, and ate the eggs raw. They were strong, but they kept him going. When he crossed the Arctic Circle, he found the Hudson Bay Company's post. The brigade had not yet arrived from the Mackenzie, and the post was completely out of grub. He was offered wild-duck eggs, but he informed them that he had a bushel of the same on the boat. He was also offered a drink of whisky, which he refused with an exhibition of violent repugnance. He got matches, however, and after that he cooked his eggs. Toward the mouth of the river head-winds delayed him, and he was twenty-four days on the egg diet. Unfortunately, while asleep he had drifted by both the missions of St. Paul and Holy Cross. And he could sincerely say, as he afterward did, that talk about missions on the Yukon was all humbug. There weren't any missions, and he was the man to know.

Once on Bering Sea he exchanged the egg diet for seal diet, and he never could make up his mind which he liked least. In the fall of the year he was rescued by a United States revenue cutter, and the following winter he made quite a hit in San Francisco as a temperance lecturer. In this field he found his vocation. "Avoid the bottle" is his slogan and battle-cry. He manages subtly to convey the impression that in his own life a great disaster was wrought by the bottle. He has even mentioned the loss of a fortune that was caused by that hell-bait of the devil, but behind that incident his listeners feel the loom of some terrible and unguessed evil for which the bottle is responsible. He has made a success in his vocation, and has grown grey and respected in the crusade against strong drink. But on the Yukon the passing of Marcus O'Brien remains tradition. It is a mystery that ranks at par with the disappearance of Sir John Franklin.

The Wit of Porportuk

E l-Soo had been a Mission girl. Her mother had died when she was very small, and Sister Alberta had plucked El-Soo as a brand from the burning, one summer day, and carried her away to Holy Cross Mission and dedicated her to God. El-Soo was a full-blooded Indian, yet she exceeded all the half-breed and quarter-breed girls. Never had the good sisters dealt with a girl so adaptable and at the same time so spirited.

El-Soo was quick, and deft, and intelligent; but above all she was fire, the living flame of life, a blaze of personality that was compounded of will, sweetness, and daring. Her father was a chief, and his blood ran in her veins. Obedience, on the part of El-Soo, was a matter of terms and arrangement. She had a passion for equity, and perhaps it was because of this that she excelled in mathematics.

But she excelled in other things. She learned to read and write English as no girl had ever learned in the Mission. She led the girls in singing, and into song she carried her sense of equity. She was an artist, and the fire of her flowed toward creation. Had she from birth enjoyed a more favourable environment, she would have made literature or music.

Instead, she was El-Soo, daughter of Klakee-Nah, a chief, and she lived in the Holy Cross Mission where were no artists, but only pure-souled Sisters who were interested in cleanliness and righteousness and the welfare of the spirit in the land of immortality that lay beyond the skies.

The years passed. She was eight years old when she entered the Mission; she was sixteen, and the Sisters were corresponding with their superiors in the Order concerning the sending of El-Soo to the United States to complete her education, when a man of her own tribe arrived at Holy Cross and had talk with her. El-Soo was somewhat appalled by him. He was dirty. He was a Caliban-like creature, primitively ugly, with a mop of hair that had never been combed. He looked at her disapprovingly and refused to sit down.

"Thy brother is dead," he said shortly.

El-Soo was not particularly shocked. She remembered little of her brother. "Thy father is an old man, and alone," the messenger went on. "His house is large and empty, and he would hear thy voice and look upon thee."

Him she remembered—Klakee-Nah, the headman of the village, the friend of the missionaries and the traders, a large man thewed like a giant, with kindly eyes and masterful ways, and striding with a consciousness of crude royalty in his carriage.

"Tell him that I will come," was El-Soo's answer.

Much to the despair of the Sisters, the brand plucked from the burning went back to the burning. All pleading with El-Soo was vain. There was much argument, expostulation, and weeping. Sister Alberta even revealed to her the project of sending her to the United States. El-Soo stared wide-eyed into the golden vista thus opened up to her, and shook her head. In her eyes persisted another vista. It was the mighty curve of the Yukon at Tana-naw Station. With the St. George Mission on one side, and the trading post on the other, and midway between the Indian village and a certain large log house where lived an old man tended upon by slaves.

All dwellers on the Yukon bank for twice a thousand miles knew the large log house, the old man and the tending slaves; and well did the Sisters know the house, its unending revelry, its feasting and its fun. So there was weeping at Holy Cross when El-Soo departed.

There was a great cleaning up in the large house when El-Soo arrived. Klakee-Nah, himself masterful, protested at this masterful conduct of his young daughter; but in the end, dreaming barbarically of magnificence, he went forth and borrowed a thousand dollars from old Porportuk, than whom there was no richer Indian on the Yukon. Also, Klakee-Nah ran up a heavy bill at the trading post. El-Soo re-created the large house. She invested it with new splendour, while Klakee-Nah maintained its ancient traditions of hospitality and revelry.

All this was unusual for a Yukon Indian, but Klakee-Nah was an unusual Indian. Not alone did he like to render inordinate hospitality, but, what of being a chief and of acquiring much money, he was able to do it. In the primitive trading days he had been a power over his people, and he had dealt profitably with the white trading companies. Later on, with Porportuk, he had made a gold-strike on the Koyokuk River. Klakee-Nah was by training and nature an aristocrat. Porportuk was bourgeois, and Porportuk bought him out of the gold-mine. Porportuk was content to plod and accumulate. Klakee-Nah went back to his large house and proceeded to spend. Porportuk was known as the richest Indian in Alaska. Klakee-Nah was known as the whitest. Porportuk was a money-lender and a usurer. Klakee-Nah was an anachronism—a mediæval ruin, a fighter and a feaster, happy with wine and song.

El-Soo adapted herself to the large house and its ways as readily as she had adapted herself to Holy Cross Mission and its ways. She did not try to reform her father and direct his footsteps toward God. It is true, she reproved him when he drank overmuch and profoundly, but that was for the sake of his health and the direction of his footsteps on solid earth.

The latchstring to the large house was always out. What with the coming and the going, it was never still. The rafters of the great living-room shook with the roar of wassail and of song. At table sat men from all the world and chiefs from distant tribes—Englishmen and Colonials, lean Yankee traders and rotund officials of the great companies, cowboys from the Western ranges, sailors from the sea, hunters and dog-mushers of a score of nationalities.

El-Soo drew breath in a cosmopolitan atmosphere. She could speak English as well as she could her native tongue, and she sang English songs and ballads. The passing Indian ceremonials she knew, and the perishing traditions. The tribal dress of the daughter of a chief she knew how to wear upon occasion. But for the most part she dressed as white women dress. Not for nothing was her needlework at the Mission and her innate artistry. She carried her clothes like a white woman, and she made clothes that could be so carried.

In her way she was as unusual as her father, and the position she occupied was as unique as his. She was the one Indian woman who was the social equal with the several white women at Tana-naw Station. She was the one Indian woman to whom white men honourably made proposals of marriage. And she was the one Indian woman whom no white man ever insulted.

For El-Soo was beautiful—not as white women are beautiful, not as Indian women are beautiful. It was the flame of her, that did not depend upon feature, that was her beauty. So far as mere line and feature went, she was the classic Indian type. The black hair and the fine bronze were hers, and the black eyes, brilliant and bold, keen as sword-light, proud; and hers the delicate eagle nose with the thin, quivering nostrils, the high cheek-bones that were not broad apart, and the thin lips that were not too thin. But over all and through all poured the flame of her—the unanalysable something that was fire and that was the soul of her, that lay mellow-warm or blazed in her eyes, that sprayed the cheeks of her, that distended the nostrils, that curled the lips, or, when the lip was in repose, that was still there in the lip, the lip palpitant with its presence.

And El-Soo had wit—rarely sharp to hurt, yet quick to search out forgivable weakness. The laughter of her mind played like lambent flame over all about her, and from all about her arose answering laughter. Yet she was never the centre of things. This she would not permit. The large house, and all of which it was significant, was her father's; and through it, to the last, moved his heroic figure—host, master of the revels, and giver of the law. It is true, as the strength oozed from him, that she caught up responsibilities from his failing hands. But in appearance he still ruled, dozing, ofttimes at the board, a bacchanalian ruin, yet in all seeming the ruler of the feast.

And through the large house moved the figure of Porportuk, ominous, with shaking head, coldly disapproving, paying for it all. Not that he really paid, for he compounded interest in weird ways, and year by year absorbed the properties of Klakee-Nah. Porportuk once took it upon himself to chide El-Soo upon the wasteful way of life in the large house—it was when he had about absorbed the last of Klakee-Nah's wealth—but he never ventured so to chide again. El-Soo, like her father, was an aristocrat, as disdainful of money as he, and with an equal sense of honour as finely strung.

Porportuk continued grudgingly to advance money, and ever the money flowed in golden foam away. Upon one thing El-Soo was resolved—her father should die as he had lived. There should be for him no passing from high to low, no diminution of the revels, no lessening of the lavish hospitality. When there was famine, as of old, the Indians came groaning to the large house and went away content. When there was famine and no money, money was borrowed from Porportuk, and the Indians still went away content. El-Soo might well have repeated, after the aristocrats of another time and place, that after her came the deluge. In her case the deluge was old Porportuk. With every advance of money, he looked upon her with a more possessive eye, and felt bourgeoning within him ancient fires.

But El-Soo had no eyes for him. Nor had she eyes for the white men who wanted to marry her at the Mission with ring and priest and book. For at Tana-naw Station was a young man, Akoon, of her own blood, and tribe, and village. He was strong and beautiful to her eyes, a great hunter, and, in that he had wandered far and much, very poor; he had been to all the unknown wastes and places; he had journeyed to

Sitka and to the United States; he had crossed the continent to Hudson Bay and back again, and as seal-hunter on a ship he had sailed to Siberia and for Japan.

When he returned from the gold-strike in Klondike he came, as was his wont, to the large house to make report to old Klakee-Nah of all the world that he had seen; and there he first saw El-Soo, three years back from the Mission. Thereat, Akoon wandered no more. He refused a wage of twenty dollars a day as pilot on the big steamboats. He hunted some and fished some, but never far from Tana-naw Station, and he was at the large house often and long. And El-Soo measured him against many men and found him good. He sang songs to her, and was ardent and glowed until all Tana-naw Station knew he loved her. And Porportuk but grinned and advanced more money for the upkeep of the large house.

Then came the death table of Klakee-Nah.

He sat at feast, with death in his throat, that he could not drown with wine. And laughter and joke and song went around, and Akoon told a story that made the rafters echo. There were no tears or sighs at that table. It was no more than fit that Klakee-Nah should die as he had lived, and none knew this better than El-Soo, with her artist sympathy. The old roystering crowd was there, and, as of old, three frost-bitten sailors were there, fresh from the long traverse from the Arctic, survivors of a ship's company of seventy-four. At Klakee-Nah's back were four old men, all that were left him of the slaves of his youth. With rheumy eyes they saw to his needs, with palsied hands filling his glass or striking him on the back between the shoulders when death stirred and he coughed and gasped.

It was a wild night, and as the hours passed and the fun laughed and roared along, death stirred more restlessly in Klakee-Nah's throat. Then it was that he sent for Porportuk. And Porportuk came in from the outside frost to look with disapproving eyes upon the meat and wine on the table for which he had paid. But as he looked down the length of flushed faces to the far end and saw the face of El-Soo, the light in his eyes flared up, and for a moment the disapproval vanished.

Place was made for him at Klakee-Nah's side, and a glass placed before him. Klakee-Nah, with his own hands, filled the glass with fervent spirits. "Drink!" he cried. "Is it not good?"

And Porportuk's eyes watered as he nodded his head and smacked his lips.

"When, in your own house, have you had such drink?" Klakee-Nah demanded.

"I will not deny that the drink is good to this old throat of mine," Porportuk made answer, and hesitated for the speech to complete the thought.

"But it costs overmuch," Klakee-Nah roared, completing it for him.

Porportuk winced at the laughter that went down the table. His eyes burned malevolently. "We were boys together, of the same age," he said. "In your throat is death. I am still alive and strong."

An ominous murmur arose from the company. Klakee-Nah coughed and strangled, and the old slaves smote him between the shoulders. He emerged gasping, and waved his hand to still the threatening rumble.

"You have grudged the very fire in your house because the wood cost overmuch!" he cried. "You have grudged life. To live cost overmuch, and you have refused to pay the price. Your life has been like a cabin where the fire is out and there are no blankets on the floor." He signalled to a slave to fill his glass, which he held aloft. "But I have lived. And I have been warm with life as you have never been warm. It is true, you shall live long. But the longest nights are the cold nights when a man shivers and lies awake. My nights have been short, but I have slept warm."

He drained the glass. The shaking hand of a slave failed to catch it as it crashed to the floor. Klakee-Nah sank back, panting, watching the upturned glasses at the lips of the drinkers, his own lips slightly smiling to the applause. At a sign, two slaves attempted to help him sit upright again. But they were weak, his frame was mighty, and the four old men tottered and shook as they helped him forward.

"But manner of life is neither here nor there," he went on. "We have other business, Porportuk, you and I, to-night. Debts are mischances, and I am in mischance with you. What of my debt, and how great is it?"

Porportuk searched in his pouch and brought forth a memorandum. He sipped at his glass and began. "There is the note of August, 1889, for three hundred dollars. The interest has never been paid. And the note of the next year for five hundred dollars. This note was included in the note of two months later for a thousand dollars. Then there is the note—"

"Never mind the many notes!" Klakee-Nah cried out impatiently. "They make my head go around and all the things inside my head. The whole! The round whole! How much is it?"

Porportuk referred to his memorandum. "Fifteen thousand nine hundred and sixty-seven dollars and seventy-five cents," he read with careful precision.

"Make it sixteen thousand, make it sixteen thousand," Klakee-Nah said grandly. "Odd numbers were ever a worry. And now—and it is for this that I have sent for you—make me out a new note for sixteen thousand, which I shall sign. I have no thought of the interest. Make it as large as you will, and make it payable in the next world, when I shall meet you by the fire of the Great Father of all Indians. Then the note will be paid. This I promise you. It is the word of Klakee-Nah."

Porportuk looked perplexed, and loudly the laughter arose and shook the room. Klakee-Nah raised his hands. "Nay," he cried. "It is not a joke. I but speak in fairness. It was for this I sent for you, Porportuk. Make out the note."

"I have no dealings with the next world," Porportuk made answer slowly.

"Have you no thought to meet me before the Great Father!" Klakee-Nah demanded. Then he added, "I shall surely be there."

"I have no dealings with the next world," Porportuk repeated sourly.

The dying man regarded him with frank amazement.

"I know naught of the next world," Porportuk explained. "I do business in this world."

Klakee-Nah's face cleared. "This comes of sleeping cold of nights," he laughed. He pondered for a space, then said, "It is in this world that you must be paid. There remains to me this house. Take it, and burn the debt in the candle there."

"It is an old house and not worth the money," Porportuk made answer.

"There are my mines on the Twisted Salmon."

"They have never paid to work," was the reply.

"There is my share in the steamer *Koyokuk*. I am half owner."

"She is at the bottom of the Yukon."

Klakee-Nah started. "True, I forgot. It was last spring when the ice went out." He mused for a time while the glasses remained untasted, and all the company waited upon his utterance.

"Then it would seem I owe you a sum of money which I cannot pay. . . in this world?" Porportuk nodded and glanced down the table.

"Then it would seem that you, Porportuk, are a poor business man," Klakee-Nah said slyly. And boldly Porportuk made answer, "No; there is security yet untouched."

"What!" cried Klakee-Nah. "Have I still property? Name it, and it is yours, and the debt is no more."

"There it is." Porportuk pointed at El-Soo.

Klakee-Nah could not understand. He peered down the table, brushed his eyes, and peered again.

"Your daughter, El-Soo—her will I take and the debt be no more. I will burn the debt there in the candle."

Klakee-Nah's great chest began to heave. "Ho! ho!—a joke. Ho! ho! ho!" he laughed Homerically. "And with your cold bed and daughters old enough to be the mother of El-Soo! Ho! ho! ho!" He began to cough and strangle, and the old slaves smote him on the back. "Ho! ho!" he began again, and went off into another paroxysm.

Porportuk waited patiently, sipping from his glass and studying the double row of faces down the board. "It is no joke," he said finally. "My speech is well meant."

Klakee-Nah sobered and looked at him, then reached for his glass, but could not touch it. A slave passed it to him, and glass and liquor he flung into the face of Porportuk.

"Turn him out!" Klakee-Nah thundered to the waiting table that strained like a pack of hounds in leash. "And roll him in the snow!"

As the mad riot swept past him and out of doors, he signalled to the slaves, and the four tottering old men supported him on his feet as he met the returning revellers, upright, glass in hand, pledging them a toast to the short night when a man sleeps warm.

It did not take long to settle the estate of Klakee-Nah. Tommy, the little Englishman, clerk at the trading post, was called in by El-Soo to help. There was nothing but debts, notes overdue, mortgaged properties, and properties mortgaged but worthless. Notes and mortgages were held by Porportuk. Tommy called him a robber many times as he pondered the compounding of the interest.

"Is it a debt, Tommy?" El-Soo asked.

"It is a robbery," Tommy answered.

"Nevertheless, it is a debt," she persisted.

The winter wore away, and the early spring, and still the claims of Porportuk remained unpaid. He saw El-Soo often and explained to her at length, as he had explained to her father, the way the debt could be cancelled. Also, he brought with him old medicine-men, who elaborated to her the everlasting damnation of her father if the debt were not paid. One day, after such an elaboration, El-Soo made final announcement to Porportuk.

"I shall tell you two things," she said. "First I shall not be your wife.

Will you remember that? Second, you shall be paid the last cent of the sixteen thousand dollars—"

"Fifteen thousand nine hundred and sixty-seven dollars and seventy-five cents," Porportuk corrected.

"My father said sixteen thousand," was her reply. "You shall be paid."

"How?"

"I know not how, but I shall find out how. Now go, and bother me no more. If you do"—she hesitated to find fitting penalty—"if you do, I shall have you rolled in the snow again as soon as the first snow flies."

This was still in the early spring, and a little later El-Soo surprised the country. Word went up and down the Yukon from Chilcoot to the Delta, and was carried from camp to camp to the farthermost camps, that in June, when the first salmon ran, El-Soo, daughter of Klakee-Nah, would sell herself at public auction to satisfy the claims of Porportuk. Vain were the attempts to dissuade her. The missionary at St. George wrestled with her, but she replied—

"Only the debts to God are settled in the next world. The debts of men are of this world, and in this world are they settled."

Akoon wrestled with her, but she replied, "I do love thee, Akoon; but honour is greater than love, and who am I that I should blacken my father?" Sister Alberta journeyed all the way up from Holy Cross on the first steamer, and to no better end.

"My father wanders in the thick and endless forests," said El-Soo. "And there will he wander, with the lost souls crying, till the debt be paid. Then, and not until then, may he go on to the house of the Great Father."

"And you believe this?" Sister Alberta asked.

"I do not know," El-Soo made answer. "It was my father's belief."

Sister Alberta shrugged her shoulders incredulously.

"Who knows but that the things we believe come true?" El-Soo went on. "Why not? The next world to you may be heaven and harps. . . because you have believed heaven and harps; to my father the next world may be a large house where he will sit always at table feasting with God."

"And you?" Sister Alberta asked. "What is your next world?"

El-Soo hesitated but for a moment. "I should like a little of both," she said. "I should like to see your face as well as the face of my father."

The day of the auction came. Tana-naw Station was populous. As was their custom, the tribes had gathered to await the salmon-run, and in the meantime spent the time in dancing and frolicking, trading and gossiping. Then there was the ordinary sprinkling of white adventurers, traders, and prospectors, and, in addition, a large number of white men who had come because of curiosity or interest in the affair.

It had been a backward spring, and the salmon were late in running. This delay but keyed up the interest. Then, on the day of the auction, the situation was made tense by Akoon. He arose and made public and solemn announcement that whosoever bought El-Soo would forthwith and immediately die. He flourished the Winchester in his hand to indicate the manner of the taking-off. El-Soo was angered thereat; but he refused to speak with her, and went to the trading post to lay in extra ammunition.

The first salmon was caught at ten o'clock in the evening, and at midnight the auction began. It took place on top of the high bank alongside the Yukon. The sun was due north just below the horizon, and the sky was lurid red. A great crowd gathered about the table and the two chairs that stood near the edge of the bank. To the fore were many white men and several chiefs. And most prominently to the fore, rifle in hand, stood Akoon. Tommy, at El-Soo's request, served as auctioneer, but she made the opening speech and described the goods about to be sold. She was in native costume, in the dress of a chief's daughter, splendid and barbaric, and she stood on a chair, that she might be seen to advantage.

"Who will buy a wife?" she asked. "Look at me. I am twenty years old and a maid. I will be a good wife to the man who buys me. If he is a white man, I shall dress in the fashion of white women; if he is an Indian, I shall dress as"—she hesitated a moment—"a squaw. I can make my own clothes, and sew, and wash, and mend. I was taught for eight years to do these things at Holy Cross Mission. I can read and write English, and I know how to play the organ. Also I can do arithmetic and some algebra—a little. I shall be sold to the highest bidder, and to him I will make out a bill of sale of myself. I forgot to say that I can sing very well, and that I have never been sick in my life. I weigh one hundred and thirty-two pounds; my father is dead and I have no relatives. Who wants me?"

She looked over the crowd with flaming audacity and stepped down. At Tommy's request she stood upon the chair again, while he mounted the second chair and started the bidding.

Surrounding El-Soo stood the four old slaves of her father. They were age-twisted and palsied, faithful to their meat, a generation out of the past that watched unmoved the antics of younger life. In the front of the crowd were several Eldorado and Bonanza kings from the Upper Yukon, and beside them, on crutches, swollen with scurvy, were two broken prospectors. From the midst of the crowd, thrust out by its own vividness, appeared the face of a wild-eyed squaw from the remote regions of the Upper Tana-naw; a strayed Sitkan from the coast stood side by side with a Stick from Lake Le Barge, and, beyond, a half-dozen French-Canadian voyageurs, grouped by themselves. From afar came the faint cries of myriads of wild-fowl on the nesting-grounds. Swallows were skimming up overhead from the placid surface of the Yukon, and robins were singing. The oblique rays of the hidden sun shot through the smoke, high-dissipated from forest fires a thousand miles away, and turned the heavens to sombre red, while the earth shone red in the reflected glow. This red glow shone in the faces of all, and made everything seem unearthly and unreal.

The bidding began slowly. The Sitkan, who was a stranger in the land and who had arrived only half an hour before, offered one hundred dollars in a confident voice, and was surprised when Akoon turned threateningly upon him with the rifle. The bidding dragged. An Indian from the Tozikakat, a pilot, bid one hundred and fifty, and after some time a gambler, who had been ordered out of the Upper Country, raised the bid to two hundred. El-Soo was saddened; her pride was hurt; but the only effect was that she flamed more audaciously upon the crowd.

There was a disturbance among the onlookers as Porportuk forced his way to the front. "Five hundred dollars!" he bid in a loud voice, then looked about him proudly to note the effect.

He was minded to use his great wealth as a bludgeon with which to stun all competition at the start. But one of the voyageurs, looking on El-Soo with sparkling eyes, raised the bid a hundred.

"Seven hundred!" Porportuk returned promptly.

And with equal promptness came the "Eight hundred" of the voyageur.

Then Porportuk swung his club again.

"Twelve hundred!" he shouted.

With a look of poignant disappointment, the voyageur succumbed. There was no further bidding. Tommy worked hard, but could not elicit a bid.

El-Soo spoke to Porportuk. "It were good, Porportuk, for you to weigh well your bid. Have you forgotten the thing I told you—that I would never marry you!"

"It is a public auction," he retorted. "I shall buy you with a bill of sale. I have offered twelve hundred dollars. You come cheap."

"Too damned cheap!" Tommy cried. "What if I am auctioneer? That does not prevent me from bidding. I'll make it thirteen hundred."

"Fourteen hundred," from Porportuk.

"I'll buy you in to be my—my sister," Tommy whispered to El-Soo, then called aloud, "Fifteen hundred!"

At two thousand one of the Eldorado kings took a hand, and Tommy dropped out.

A third time Porportuk swung the club of his wealth, making a clean raise of five hundred dollars. But the Eldorado king's pride was touched. No man could club him. And he swung back another five hundred.

El-Soo stood at three thousand. Porportuk made it thirty-five hundred, and gasped when the Eldorado king raised it a thousand dollars. Porportuk again raised it five hundred, and again gasped when the king raised a thousand more.

Porportuk became angry. His pride was touched; his strength was challenged, and with him strength took the form of wealth. He would not be ashamed for weakness before the world. El-Soo became incidental. The savings and scrimpings from the cold nights of all his years were ripe to be squandered. El-Soo stood at six thousand. He made it seven thousand. And then, in thousand-dollar bids, as fast as they could be uttered, her price went up. At fourteen thousand the two men stopped for breath.

Then the unexpected happened. A still heavier club was swung. In the pause that ensued, the gambler, who had scented a speculation and formed a syndicate with several of his fellows, bid sixteen thousand dollars.

"Seventeen thousand," Porportuk said weakly.

"Eighteen thousand," said the king.

Porportuk gathered his strength. "Twenty thousand."

The syndicate dropped out. The Eldorado king raised a thousand, and Porportuk raised back; and as they bid, Akoon turned from one to the other, half menacingly, half curiously, as though to see what manner of man it was that he would have to kill. When the king prepared to make his next bid, Akoon having pressed closer, the king first loosed the revolver at his hip, then said:

"Twenty-three thousand."

"Twenty-four thousand," said Porportuk. He grinned viciously, for the certitude of his bidding had at last shaken the king. The latter moved over close to El-Soo. He studied her carefully for a long while.

"And five hundred," he said at last.

"Twenty-five thousand," came Porportuk's raise.

The king looked for a long space, and shook his head. He looked again, and said reluctantly, "And five hundred."

"Twenty-six thousand," Porportuk snapped.

The king shook his head and refused to meet Tommy's pleading eye. In the meantime Akoon had edged close to Porportuk. El-Soo's quick eye noted this, and, while Tommy wrestled with the Eldorado king for another bid, she bent, and spoke in a low voice in the ear of a slave. And while Tommy's "Going—going—going—" dominated the air, the slave went up to Akoon and spoke in a low voice in his ear. Akoon made no sign that he had heard, though El-Soo watched him anxiously.

"Gone!" Tommy's voice rang out. "To Porportuk, for twenty-six thousand dollars."

Porportuk glanced uneasily at Akoon. All eyes were centred upon Akoon, but he did nothing.

"Let the scales be brought," said El-Soo.

"I shall make payment at my house," said Porportuk.

"Let the scales be brought," El-Soo repeated. "Payment shall be made here where all can see."

So the gold scales were brought from the trading post, while Porportuk went away and came back with a man at his heels, on whose shoulders was a weight of gold-dust in moose-hide sacks. Also, at Porportuk's back, walked another man with a rifle, who had eyes only for Akoon.

"Here are the notes and mortgages," said Porportuk, "for fifteen thousand nine hundred and sixty-seven dollars and seventy-five cents."

El-Soo received them into her hands and said to Tommy, "Let them be reckoned as sixteen thousand."

"There remains ten thousand dollars to be paid in gold," Tommy said.

Porportuk nodded, and untied the mouths of the sacks. El-Soo, standing at the edge of the bank, tore the papers to shreds and sent them fluttering out over the Yukon. The weighing began, but halted.

"Of course, at seventeen dollars," Porportuk had said to Tommy, as he adjusted the scales.

"At sixteen dollars," El-Soo said sharply.

"It is the custom of all the land to reckon gold at seventeen dollars for each ounce," Porportuk replied. "And this is a business transaction."

El-Soo laughed. "It is a new custom," she said. "It began this spring. Last year, and the years before, it was sixteen dollars an ounce. When my father's debt was made, it was sixteen dollars. When he spent at the store the money he got from you, for one ounce he was given sixteen dollars' worth of flour, not seventeen. Wherefore, shall you pay for me at sixteen, and not at seventeen." Porportuk grunted and allowed the weighing to proceed.

"Weigh it in three piles, Tommy," she said. "A thousand dollars here, three thousand here, and here six thousand."

It was slow work, and, while the weighing went on, Akoon was closely watched by all.

"He but waits till the money is paid," one said; and the word went around and was accepted, and they waited for what Akoon should do when the money was paid. And Porportuk's man with the rifle waited and watched Akoon.

The weighing was finished, and the gold-dust lay on the table in three dark-yellow heaps. "There is a debt of my father to the Company for three thousand dollars," said El-Soo. "Take it, Tommy, for the Company. And here are four old men, Tommy. You know them. And here is one thousand dollars. Take it, and see that the old men are never hungry and never without tobacco."

Tommy scooped the gold into separate sacks. Six thousand dollars remained on the table. El-Soo thrust the scoop into the heap, and with a sudden turn whirled the contents out and down to the Yukon in a golden shower. Porportuk seized her wrist as she thrust the scoop a second time into the heap.

"It is mine," she said calmly. Porportuk released his grip, but he gritted his teeth and scowled darkly as she continued to scoop the gold into the river till none was left.

The crowd had eyes for naught but Akoon, and the rifle of Porportuk's man lay across the hollow of his arm, the muzzle directed at Akoon a yard away, the man's thumb on the hammer. But Akoon did nothing.

"Make out the bill of sale," Porportuk said grimly.

And Tommy made out the till of sale, wherein all right and title in the woman El-Soo was vested in the man Porportuk. El-Soo signed the document, and Porportuk folded it and put it away in his pouch. Suddenly his eyes flashed, and in sudden speech he addressed El-Soo.

"But it was not your father's debt," he said, "What I paid was the price for you. Your sale is business of to-day and not of last year and the years before. The ounces paid for you will buy at the post to-day seventeen dollars of flour, and not sixteen. I have lost a dollar on each ounce. I have lost six hundred and twenty-five dollars."

El-Soo thought for a moment, and saw the error she had made. She smiled, and then she laughed.

"You are right," she laughed, "I made a mistake. But it is too late. You have paid, and the gold is gone. You did not think quick. It is your loss. Your wit is slow these days, Porportuk. You are getting old."

He did not answer. He glanced uneasily at Akoon, and was reassured. His lips tightened, and a hint of cruelty came into his face. "Come," he said, "we will go to my house."

"Do you remember the two things I told you in the spring?" El-Soo asked, making no movement to accompany him.

"My head would be full with the things women say, did I heed them," he answered.

"I told you that you would be paid," El-Soo went on carefully. "And I told you that I would never be your wife."

"But that was before the bill of sale." Porportuk crackled the paper between his fingers inside the pouch. "I have bought you before all the world. You belong to me. You will not deny that you belong to me."

"I belong to you," El-Soo said steadily.

"I own you."

"You own me."

Porportuk's voice rose slightly and triumphantly. "As a dog, I own you."

"As a dog you own me," El-Soo continued calmly. "But, Porportuk, you forget the thing I told you. Had any other man bought me, I should have been that man's wife. I should have been a good wife to that man. Such was my will. But my will with you was that I should never be your wife. Wherefore, I am your dog."

Porportuk knew that he played with fire, and he resolved to play firmly. "Then I speak to you, not as El-Soo, but as a dog," he said; "and I tell you to come with me." He half reached to grip her arm, but with a gesture she held him back.

"Not so fast, Porportuk. You buy a dog. The dog runs away. It is your loss. I am your dog. What if I run away?"

"As the owner of the dog, I shall beat you—"

"When you catch me?"

"When I catch you."

"Then catch me."

He reached swiftly for her, but she eluded him. She laughed as she circled around the table. "Catch her!" Porportuk commanded the Indian with the rifle, who stood near to her. But as the Indian stretched forth his arm to her, the Eldorado king felled him with a fist blow under the ear. The rifle clattered to the ground. Then was Akoon's chance. His eyes glittered, but he did nothing.

Porportuk was an old man, but his cold nights retained for him his activity. He did not circle the table. He came across suddenly, over the top of the table. El-Soo was taken off her guard. She sprang back with a sharp cry of alarm, and Porportuk would have caught her had it not been for Tommy. Tommy's leg went out, Porportuk tripped and pitched forward on the ground. El-Soo got her start.

"Then catch me," she laughed over her shoulder, as she fled away.

She ran lightly and easily, but Porportuk ran swiftly and savagely. He outran her. In his youth he had been swiftest of all the young men. But El-Soo dodged in a willowy, elusive way. Being in native dress, her feet were not cluttered with skirts, and her pliant body curved a flight that defied the gripping fingers of Porportuk.

With laughter and tumult, the great crowd scattered out to see the chase. It led through the Indian encampment; and ever dodging, circling, and reversing, El-Soo and Porportuk appeared and disappeared among the tents. El-Soo seemed to balance herself against the air with her arms, now one side, now on the other, and sometimes her body, too, leaned out upon the air far from the perpendicular as she achieved her sharpest curves. And Porportuk, always a leap behind, or a leap this side or that, like a lean hound strained after her.

They crossed the open ground beyond the encampment and disappeared in the forest. Tana-naw Station waited their reappearance, and long and vainly it waited.

In the meantime Akoon ate and slept, and lingered much at the steamboat landing, deaf to the rising resentment of Tana-naw Station in that he did nothing. Twenty-four hours later Porportuk returned. He was tired and savage. He spoke to no one but Akoon, and with him tried to pick a quarrel. But Akoon shrugged his shoulders and walked away. Porportuk did not waste time. He outfitted half a dozen of the young men, selecting the best trackers and travellers, and at their head plunged into the forest.

Next day the steamer *Seattle*, bound up river, pulled in to the shore and wooded up. When the lines were cast off and she churned out from the bank, Akoon was on board in the pilot-house. Not many hours afterward, when it was his turn at the wheel, he saw a small birch-bark canoe put off from the shore. There was only one person in it. He studied it carefully, put the wheel over, and slowed down.

The captain entered the pilot-house. "What's the matter?" he demanded. "The water's good."

Akoon grunted. He saw a larger canoe leaving the bank, and in it were a number of persons. As the *Seattle* lost headway, he put the wheel over some more.

The captain fumed. "It's only a squaw," he protested.

Akoon did not grunt. He was all eyes for the squaw and the pursuing canoe. In the latter six paddles were flashing, while the squaw paddled slowly.

"You'll be aground," the captain protested, seizing the wheel.

But Akoon countered his strength on the wheel and looked him in the eyes. The captain slowly released the spokes.

"Queer beggar," he sniffed to himself.

Akoon held the *Seattle* on the edge of the shoal water and waited till he saw the squaw's fingers clutch the forward rail. Then he signalled for full speed ahead and ground the wheel over. The large canoe was very near, but the gap between it and the steamer was widening.

The squaw laughed and leaned over the rail.

"Then catch me, Porportuk!" she cried.

Akoon left the steamer at Fort Yukon. He outfitted a small poling-boat and went up the Porcupine River. And with him went El-Soo. It was a weary journey, and the way led across the backbone of the world; but Akoon had travelled it before. When they came to the head-waters of the Porcupine, they left the boat and went on foot across the Rocky Mountains.

Akoon greatly liked to walk behind El-Soo and watch the movements of her. There was a music in it that he loved. And especially he loved the well-rounded calves in their sheaths of soft-tanned leather, the slim ankles, and the small moccasined feet that were tireless through the longest days.

"You are light as air," he said, looking up at her. "It is no labour for you to walk. You almost float, so lightly do your feet rise and fall. You are like a deer, El-Soo; you are like a deer, and your eyes are like deer's eyes, sometimes when you look at me, or when you hear a quick sound and wonder if it be danger that stirs. Your eyes are like a deer's eyes now as you look at me."

And El-Soo, luminous and melting, bent and kissed Akoon.

"When we reach the Mackenzie, we will not delay," Akoon said later. "We will go south before the winter catches us. We will go to the sunlands where there is no snow. But we will return. I have seen much of the world, and there is no land like Alaska, no sun like our sun, and the snow is good after the long summer."

"And you will learn to read," said El-Soo.

And Akoon said, "I will surely learn to read." But there was delay when they reached the Mackenzie. They fell in with a band of Mackenzie Indians, and, hunting, Akoon was shot by accident. The rifle was in the hands of a youth. The bullet broke Akoon's right arm and, ranging farther, broke two of his ribs. Akoon knew rough surgery, while El-Soo had learned some refinements at Holy Cross. The bones were finally set, and Akoon lay by the fire for them to knit. Also, he lay by the fire so that the smoke would keep the mosquitoes away.

Then it was that Porportuk, with his six young men, arrived. Akoon groaned in his helplessness and made appeal to the Mackenzies. But Porportuk made demand, and the Mackenzies were perplexed. Porportuk was for seizing upon El-Soo, but this they would not permit. Judgment must be given, and, as it was an affair of man and woman, the council of the old men was called—this that warm judgment might not be given by the young men, who were warm of heart.

The old men sat in a circle about the smudge-fire. Their faces were lean and wrinkled, and they gasped and panted for air. The smoke was not good for them. Occasionally they struck with withered hands at the mosquitoes that braved the smoke. After such exertion they coughed hollowly and painfully. Some spat blood, and one of them sat a bit apart with head bowed forward, and bled slowly and continuously at the mouth; the coughing sickness had gripped them. They were as dead men; their time was short. It was a judgment of the dead.

"And I paid for her a heavy price," Porportuk concluded his complaint. "Such a price you have never seen. Sell all that is yours—sell your spears and arrows and rifles, sell your skins and furs, sell your tents and boats and dogs, sell everything, and you will not have maybe a thousand dollars. Yet did I pay for the woman, El-Soo, twenty-six times the price of all your spears and arrows and rifles, your skins and furs, your tents and boats and dogs. It was a heavy price."

The old men nodded gravely, though their weazened eye-slits widened with wonder that any woman should be worth such a price. The one that bled at the mouth wiped his lips. "Is it true talk?" he asked each of Porportuk's six young men. And each answered that it was true.

"Is it true talk?" he asked El-Soo, and she answered, "It is true."

"But Porportuk has not told that he is an old man," Akoon said, "and that he has daughters older than El-Soo."

"It is true, Porportuk is an old man," said El-Soo.

"It is for Porportuk to measure the strength his age," said he who bled at the mouth. "We be old men. Behold! Age is never so old as youth would measure it."

And the circle of old men champed their gums, and nodded approvingly, and coughed.

"I told him that I would never be his wife," said El-Soo.

"Yet you took from him twenty-six times all that we possess?" asked a one-eyed old man.

El-Soo was silent.

"It is true?" And his one eye burned and bored into her like a fiery gimlet.

"It is true," she said.

"But I will run away again," she broke out passionately, a moment later. "Always will I run away."

"That is for Porportuk to consider," said another of the old men. "It is for us to consider the judgment."

"What price did you pay for her?" was demanded of Akoon.

"No price did I pay for her," he answered. "She was above price. I did not measure her in gold-dust, nor in dogs, and tents, and furs."

The old men debated among themselves and mumbled in undertones. "These old men are ice," Akoon said in English. "I will not listen to their judgment, Porportuk. If you take El-Soo, I will surely kill you."

The old men ceased and regarded him suspiciously. "We do not know the speech you make," one said.

"He but said that he would kill me," Porportuk volunteered. "So it were well to take from him his rifle, and to have some of your young men sit by him, that he may not do me hurt. He is a young man, and what are broken bones to youth!"

Akoon, lying helpless, had rifle and knife taken from him, and to either side of his shoulders sat young men of the Mackenzies. The one-eyed old man arose and stood upright. "We marvel at the price paid for one mere woman," he began; "but the wisdom of the price is no concern of ours. We are here to give judgment, and judgment we give. We have no doubt. It is known to all that Porportuk paid a heavy price for the woman El-Soo. Wherefore does the woman El-Soo belong to Porportuk and none other." He sat down heavily, and coughed. The old men nodded and coughed.

"I will kill you," Akoon cried in English.

Porportuk smiled and stood up. "You have given true judgment," he said to the council, "and my young men will give to you much tobacco. Now let the woman be brought to me."

Akoon gritted his teeth. The young men took El-Soo by the arms. She did not resist, and was led, her face a sullen flame, to Porportuk.

"Sit there at my feet till I have made my talk," he commanded. He paused a moment. "It is true," he said, "I am an old man. Yet can I understand the ways of youth. The fire has not all gone out of me. Yet am I no longer young, nor am I minded to run these old legs of mine through all the years that remain to me. El-Soo can run fast and well. She is a deer. This I know, for I have seen and run after her. It is not good that a wife should run so fast. I paid for her a heavy price, yet does she run away from me. Akoon paid no price at all, yet does she run to him.

"When I came among you people of the Mackenzie, I was of one mind. As I listened in the council and thought of the swift legs of El-Soo, I was of many minds. Now am I of one mind again but it is a different mind from the one I brought to the council. Let me tell you my mind. When a dog runs once away from a master, it will run away again. No matter how many times it is brought back, each time it will run away again. When we have such dogs, we sell them. El-Soo is like a dog that runs away. I will sell her. Is there any man of the council that will buy?"

The old men coughed and remained silent

"Akoon would buy," Porportuk went on, "but he has no money. Wherefore I will give El-Soo to him, as he said, without price. Even now will I give her to him."

Reaching down, he took El-Soo by the hand and led her across the space to where Akoon lay on his back.

"She has a bad habit, Akoon," he said, seating her at Akoon's feet. "As she has run away from me in the past, in the days to come she may run away from you. But there is no need to fear that she will ever run away, Akoon. I shall see to that. Never will she run away from you— this is the word of Porportuk. She has great wit. I know, for often has it bitten into me. Yet am I minded myself to give my wit play for once. And by my wit will I secure her to you, Akoon."

Stooping, Porportuk crossed El-Soo's feet, so that the instep of one lay over that of the other; and then, before his purpose could be divined, he discharged his rifle through the two ankles. As Akoon struggled to rise against the weight of the young men, there was heard the crunch of the broken bone rebroken.

"It is just," said the old men, one to another.

El-Soo made no sound. She sat and looked at her shattered ankles, on which she would never walk again.

"My legs are strong, El-Soo," Akoon said. "But never will they bear me away from you."

El-Soo looked at him, and for the first time in all the time he had known her, Akoon saw tears in her eyes.

"Your eyes are like deer's eyes, El-Soo," he said.

"Is it just?" Porportuk asked, and grinned from the edge of the smoke as he prepared to depart.

"It is just," the old men said. And they sat on in the silence.

A Note About the Author

Jack London (1876–1916) was an American novelist and journalist. Born in San Francisco to Florence Wellman, a spiritualist, and William Chaney, an astrologer, London was raised by his mother and her husband, John London, in Oakland. An intelligent boy, Jack went on to study at the University of California, Berkeley before leaving school to join the Klondike Gold Rush. His experiences in the Klondike—hard labor, life in a hostile environment, and bouts of scurvy—both shaped his sociopolitical outlook and served as powerful material for such works as "To Build a Fire" (1902), *The Call of the Wild* (1903), and *White Fang* (1906). When he returned to Oakland, London embarked on a career as a professional writer, finding success with novels and short fiction. In 1904, London worked as a war correspondent covering the Russo-Japanese War and was arrested several times by Japanese authorities. Upon returning to California, he joined the famous Bohemian Club, befriending such members as Ambrose Bierce and John Muir. London married Charmian Kittredge in 1905, the same year he purchased the thousand-acre Beauty Ranch in Sonoma County, California. London, who suffered from numerous illnesses throughout his life, died on his ranch at the age of 40. A lifelong advocate for socialism and animal rights, London is recognized as a pioneer of science fiction and an important figure in twentieth century American literature.

A Note from the Publisher

Spanning many genres, from non-fiction essays to literature classics to children's books and lyric poetry, Mint Edition books showcase the master works of our time in a modern new package. The text is freshly typeset, is clean and easy to read, and features a new note about the author in each volume. Many books also include exclusive new introductory material. Every book boasts a striking new cover, which makes it as appropriate for collecting as it is for gift giving. Mint Edition books are only printed when a reader orders them, so natural resources are not wasted. We're proud that our books are never manufactured in excess and exist only in the exact quantity they need to be read and enjoyed.

bookfinity™

Discover more of your favorite classics with Bookfinity™.

- Track your reading with custom book lists.
- Get great book recommendations for your personalized Reader Type.
- Add reviews for your favorite books.
- AND MUCH MORE!

Visit **bookfinity.com** and take the fun Reader Type quiz to get started.

Enjoy our classic and modern companion pairings!

Bookfinity is a registered trademark of Ingram Book Group LLC. © 2023 Bookfinity. All rights reserved.

Printed in the USA
CPSIA information can be obtained
at www.ICGtesting.com
JSHW082146140824
68134JS00002B/5

9 781513 206523